RED FLAGS

by

Mariaelena

DORRANCE
PUBLISHING CO
EST. 1920
PITTSBURGH, PENNSYLVANIA 15238

Dorrance Publishing Co
585 Alpha Drive
Pittsburgh, PA 15238
Visit our website at www.dorrancebookstore.com

ISBN: 979-8-88729-054-6
eISBN: 979-8-88729-554-1

Dedicated to TK.
Thank you for loving me.
Thank you for healing me.
Thank you for saving me.

Chapter 1

She's lying in her bed, staring at the ceiling. He is out with his friends drinking. He will be home soon. What she wouldn't give for him to just go straight to bed when he gets home. The door unlocks and he walks in. As he continues walking, each step is like an added elephant on her chest. The bedroom door opens, she pretends to be asleep. Maybe just this once, he'll leave her be....

He takes off his clothes, swaying back and forth intoxicated, and climbs into bed.

"Wake up, baby," he whispers in her ear.

She pretends to continue sleeping.

"Wake up, baby," he says again, this time harsher.

If she doesn't wake up, things could get ugly. She pretends to slowly wake up and open her eyes. She looks at him and he's so drunk his eyes are glossed over. He's swaying in the bed too.

"Babe, I don't feel good. Can we just go back to bed?" she says, hoping he'll be nice.

He rips her around and sits on top. His breath reeks of vodka.

"You are lucky I didn't cheat on you tonight. I had plenty of girls tonight I could've cheated on you with. Do you not know how lucky you are that I remain faithful and loyal to you? I remain those things so I can come home and get your pussy whenever I want. If you are going to start rejecting me, I will have to look elsewhere. You don't want that, do you, baby?"

Maybe she does want that. She refrains from rolling her eyes and making it worse.

"No, of course I don't want that. I'm sorry, baby," she says.
"Good girl," he whispers in her ears as he inserts himself inside of her.

She just lays back and thinks of how much of an idiot she is for taking his crap. How much easier it would be to leave. Her momma didn't raise her this way....

———

Antoinette wakes up sweating. She still can feel him and smell the alcohol on his breath as if she's physically back under him and in the past. He's haunting her again. She got up and walked away the day after his birthday six years ago and yet he is still trying to control her. Will she ever truly move on and release herself from that metaphoric grip he still has on her?

"It's all in your head. He's gone," she tells herself. She looks over and sees her peaceful dogs sleeping and focuses on their breathing until she falls back asleep...

———

Meet Antoinette. Antoinette is working hard to make her dream of being a United States President or Supreme Court Justice come true. She worked a full-time job as a server in a high-scale restaurant, part-time internship working for a State Representative and was working on her bachelor's degree studying political science and pre-law. She believed herself to be a total badass. Straight A's and headed to law school. She'd work her ass off doing 14-16-hour days at both jobs and then go out and party to reward herself.

Antoinette was half Cuban and half French-Canadian—an exotic mix, if you will. She had long hair as thick as a horse's tail that she dyed bright red like Jessica Rabbit. Honey-brown eyes and olive-white skin as glow-in-the-dark as Snow White. For being part Cuban, she burned fairly easy. She had big tits and an even bigger ass that she loved to flaunt along with thick thighs and a tummy too. Not Beyonce by any means but she was beautiful and she knew it.

Every Friday was "Fondle Friday" with her best friend, AJ, downtown. They'd go out in slutty clothes, get drunk and count how many beards they could fondle (with consent, of course—no means no with men too, y'all). Then they would sober up at the casino and get breakfast with whatever cuties they met. She was living her best life.

AJ was about 1/10th of Antoinette's size and had long, beautiful blonde hair and legs that didn't quit. They met years prior at the Detroit Hoedown with mutual friends. AJ was so friendly and kind, which Antoinette was not used to, that she thought she might be a lesbian. They became friends incredibly quickly despite their differences on religion and politics. They would spend Mondays drinking half-off martinis discussing religion, politics, and everything under the sun without ever arguing or getting in a fight. They were able to have educated and meaningful conversations with different opinions and no animosity toward each other. It was a true sign of respect and trust, a sign that everyone should encompass into their life when having discussions with people they might not necessarily agree with.

Antoinette spent the last four years sticking her middle finger up to *the man* due to a previous relationship that just about ruined her life. She had a dark and ugly past with that bad man but she was sleeping her way through Detroit to forget about him. And she would only sleep with men who were emotionally unavailable...and married. The way she saw it, married men couldn't fall in love with her so she was safe. She was focusing on herself and becoming the baddest bitch she could be as future president. But she had needs. Don't judge.

While she had many good qualities, her attitude and sass will always be the one to stand out. Ask anyone and they'll say, "She's a bitch." It's true and guess what? Antoinette gave zero fucks about it. She is one of the lead trainers at Rushing Bar & Grill. She can run circles around other servers and has never had any customer complaints. She knew how to work that charm and read her customers. The cleavage never hurt either. Working in a restaurant is something everyone should do in their lifetime. It teaches you grace, money management, and shows you people's true colors. If you ever go on a date with someone who is rude to the server, that is a big red flag. Restaurants are like high schools. There are cliques, scandal, infidelity, drama and even more drama. Managers typically play favorites to whomever kisses their ass most and run servers ragged for a measly $2.65 per hour.

She walks into Rushing for her night shift after a full 9-5 shift at her internship to see this old, skinny man talking to all the servers.

I had only been gone a week to visit family in Arizona, why didn't anyone tell me about the new guy?

"Howdy, ma'am, I'm Tanner. I'm the new dishwasher."

Okay. You're weird. Who says howdy? And why are you introducing yourself to me? I didn't say hello.

She smiled that fake smile and just kept walking. Antoinette heard another server tell him, "Don't pay her any attention. Antoinette is hard around the edges but kind of nice once you get to know her." She laughed at that.

Maybe if people knew all the shit I went through in years past to get where I am, they'd understand why I was such a bitch in the first place.

————

In the following weeks, Antoinette found herself more and more irritated by this guy, *Tanner*. He was average height but skinny as hell. He had strawberry-blonde and gray hair with a semi-full beard. He was just as white as she was, only he was the definition of a redneck, his neck was literally red. She hated to admit it but Tanner did have these insanely beautiful baby-blue eyes and dimples that just didn't quit. And his laugh was really cute. But he was like 40 years old, working in a dishtank. Why? And he was so nice, everyone loved him.

He went above and beyond his job duties, sorting silverware for the servers, picking up the heavy buckets of dirty dishes for the girls (as if they cannot do it themselves), and getting ice. When Antoinette closed, she would yell at Tanner and tell him to let the girls do it. He wasn't getting paid more to do their jobs for them. Tanner would simply brush her off with his baby-blue eyes and deep dimples.

No one is this nice for no reason. Why do all this extra work? And why doesn't he tell me off whenever I am mean to him? she wondered to herself. That was the most frustrating part for her; she lived for confrontation.

It's a Saturday, and all the girls at the Rushing decided to go to The Grasshopper after work. It's right down the street from Rushing, a total dive bar. The bathrooms aren't totally sanitary but the drinks are cheap and they have karaoke. Antoinette never, ever partakes in karaoke as her mom always raised her to believe she was tone deaf but never misses an opportunity for a good laugh at others' expense.

"Yeah, I'll drive you back home after if you come. Please come, it'll be fun...," Antoinette heard Becky asking this old-ass dishwasher to come with them and her cheeks turned instantly red with anger.

First, this is supposed to be a girls' night. And two, does Becky have a crush on Tanner? I mean, I guess why not, they are around the same age.
Why did a twinge of jealousy hit her as she was thinking about Becky liking Tanner? *Shake it off, he's old and a dishwasher, for Pete's sake! You are going to be president!*

Next thing you know, she starts telling the girls that she has to run home and change before going to the Wagon Wheel, which makes absolutely no sense because they always go in their work uniforms. *All because this guy is coming? Focus on the presidency!* she tells herself while still giving in and running home to put on lipstick, deodorant and her best see-through top. Curvy chicks can wear see-through tops too. Antoinette was all about defying the social norms.

There were twelve servers in all at one long table when Antoinette walked into the bar and she instantly was hit with nausea and nervousness.

I am not here to impress Tanner..., she said to herself. *I did all of this to look good for pictures....*

Tanner walks in about an hour later and looks directly at her with those blue eyes and something deep in her groin growled with anxiety and thirst. Of course, Antoinette pretended she didn't see him and kept talking to the other girls. Another hour passed and everyone was either tipsy or full blown drunk. Antoinette was so annoyed and intrigued by him being there that she couldn't even get tipsy. Tanner was buying pitcher after pitcher of beer for the table.

Being the snob she was, she didn't drink any of it, which also could have contributed to her lack of intoxication. Her usual White Russians weren't doing the trick. This fool was taking up all of her energy.

She was deep inside the booth of the table and at least five feet from Tanner at all times. Becky was talking his ear off and everyone else was just saying how awesome he was for buying them all beer. Mooches. She felt him staring at her all night but refused to give him the satisfaction and look back. Why was this man getting under her skin so well? She hated every minute of him being there. Part of her wanted to rip his clothes off, part of her wanted to punch him in his redneck, dimple-having face.

One minute Antoinette is texting AJ about how annoyed she was and the next, Tanner slid his ass all the way in that booth and directly next to her. The other girls had gotten up to karaoke while she was mid-text and he took it upon himself to seize the moment. Bold move, Mr. Tanner. Bold move.

Instantly, Antoinette couldn't breathe. His baby-blue eyes and dimples staring right at her. He was grinning up to his eyes. He wore deep blue that complemented his fair skin, strawberry-blonde hair and baby blues. The hair on her neck stood up, and her clit was pulsating. Antoinette felt like her damn heart was nearly bumping out of her chest. Antoinette had never felt this about anyone before. *So this is what ridiculous chemistry feels like.*

"So were you just planning on ignoring me all night?" Tanner asked her, staring her dead in the face. He knew he was making her squirm and he was enjoying it.

"I'm not ignoring you. I just wasn't near you to talk," she lied. "Well, now you are. Why do you hate me?"

Damn. Those dimples when he smiled. Antoinette could have melted right into that booth with those dimples. Ever since she was fifteen she had three weaknesses: tattoos, dimples and curly hair (added beards by age 20) and if you had at least two of those traits, she was pudding in your hands.

"I don't hate you. I just think you're too nice buying people shit and doing things for everyone constantly. People aren't that genuine. Quit being an asskisser."

He laughed so loud, a deep vein in the middle of his forehead popped out, and the rest of the girls at the table turned around and stared. She turned red.

"What is so funny?" she asked, annoyed.

He simply said "You" with that sly smile and scooted closer.

She took a deep breath and he definitely noticed the rise and fall of her chest. His eyes peered down at her breast as she took that deep breath and then looked back up at her eyes with such lust. She would've fucked him right there on that booth.

They spent the rest of the night talking and drinking. All the girls kept giving Antoinette those looks. The devilish "you want to fuck him, don't you" looks. Oh, and did she. But she wasn't going to. He had kids, was divorced and a dishwasher. And old. She wasn't going down that rabbit hole, too much baggage. Besides, she didn't mess with *available* men. Too much risk.

At the end of the night, half the girls were drunken messes and could not drive home. Becky, the mom of the group, offered to drive them all home. Antoinette offered to drive Tanner home since he lived right down the street and Becky was running out of room in her car. She had a love-hate struggle going on with this choice. There was something about him just drawing her in while she just kept trying to stay away.

When he said he lived down the street, he literally could have walked. *Eye roll.* She pulled into his condo complex and parked. It's a little after two in the morning and they're both pretty buzzed. They have been talking all night at the bar and Antoinette secretly didn't want it to end. She liked talking to him, it was easy. Well, she got what she wanted. Next thing they know, it's almost 5 A.M. and they are still talking in the damn car. He's already tried to kiss her three different times and she's rejected him each time. The third time, he straight up crawled over the center console to get on top of her. She wanted so badly to give in but she refrained. Antoinette already knew at this point that she was going to fuck him. Not tonight but at some point. He was too delicious to pass up. Stupid mistake. Finally around 6 A.M., Tanner got outside to leave and asked her to get up and give him a hug.

"I don't do hugs," Antoinette told him.

But he saw right through that Great Wall of China around her heart. They were outside talking, not totally wanting him to head inside, and he just leaned her up against the car and kissed her just like you see in the damn movies. The kiss was everything. Tanner placed one hand behind her head and pulled the hair a little bit while the other grabbed her ass. Old-ass man knew what he was doing, that was for sure. She probably would have slept with him that night if he had tried. She saw fireworks during that kiss and smiled the entire way home touching her lips, trying to feel the kiss all over again. Stupid dimples and stupid blue eyes.

Chapter 2

Tanner and Antoinette still pretended to hate each other for work purposes. Antoinette still kind of hated him, regardless of his delicious lips. He was still too nice and too generous. But that hate added to the attraction, plus the not wanting to get caught added even more adrenaline. A slight butt grab here, slight wink there. Sneak off to the basement of Rushing to make out in dry storage. Texting constantly and on the phone till 4 A.M.

Summer was coming to an end and Antoinette was preparing for her last semester of undergrad. *No funny business,* she told herself. On the last Friday of the month, AJ was turning 25; Antoinette was always the baby of the group. Antoinette requested that night off for AJ's birthday and her boss at Rushing said to come in anyways or she wouldn't have a job. Little did her boss know that the internship she had been busting her ass for working for free all summer had just offered herself a paid position starting the following week. So in the heat of the moment with that ultimatum, Antoinette quit. She would have an anxiety attack about it the next day, but tonight she was celebrating her best friend turning 25.

It was a masquerade-themed party and Antoinette was bold enough to buy Tanner a mask. Why, you ask? People do stupid shit when they're smitten. "Just wear it and no one will know who you are. Besides, no one from

Rushing is coming, this is a completely different friend group." She wanted so badly for him to come. Antoinette had caught feelings even if she was refusing to admit it.

"Becky already invited me to the Wagon Wheel and I invited some of my buddies to join."

Oh, okay. Becky. Of course. Her green monster of jealousy was showing through again. She brushed him off and pushed him away that night, drinking away any feelings she had.

1:30 A.M. and she receives a text. *He probably already banged Becky,* she thought to herself. Damn, her jealousy was getting out of control.

Tanner: *I missed you tonight.*

Antoinette: *Cool.*

Tanner: *I also almost ended up in jail. Got in a fight.*

Her stomach sank. She wanted to keep acting like she didn't care but she couldn't keep up the facade.

Antoinette: *Are you okay? What happened?*

He called her.

Tanner: *Some guy wanted to start shit with my friend and I stepped in. This guy choked me out so hard, I saw my life flash before my eyes. Know what I saw at that moment? My kids. Not you. You don't even like kids. You don't want kids, you don't want marriage. What are we even doing?*

Antoinette: *Okay, rude. I like kids, I just don't want any of my own. But if you didn't think of me, then cool. We can stop this. No harm, no foul.*

And just like that, Antoinette's walls were back up.

Fuck you then. I am going to law school and becoming president. I didn't have time for that kind of drama, she thought to herself as she continued to drink for AJ's birthday. She lost a good-paying job and a sexy-ass old man all in one night. Trying to forget about him required many more shots than quitting Rushing did. Three o'clock in the morning, she received another text. Secretly Antoinette hoped it was Tanner wanting to apologize. Dazed and pretty faded, she opens up her phone and it's from a number she doesn't know.

"My sweet mamita. I miss you so much. I am sober now, I swear it. Give me another chance."

Instant panic hit Antoinette. How did he get her number? Wasn't he back in Mexico? Fuck, fuck, fuck. She quickly deleted that message and turned off her phone. Enough toxic men for one night.

———

With no longer working at Rushing, Antoinette didn't have to see Tanner. It was easy for them not to talk. And now she found a new old-ass man to have some fun with: Donny. Donny was eighteen years her senior; yes, he graduated high school the same year she was born. He was deliciously covered in tattoos from head to toe with his inside shaft and nipples pierced, but he was married so there could be no emotional attachments, which is exactly what she was looking for. She met him at Rushing shortly before she quit, he messaged her and the rest was history.

She started her last semester of undergrad, continued her Fondle Fridays with AJ and applied to law schools. She did all this while still messing around with Donny when his wife thought he was working and putting Tanner and *him* behind her. Neither of them texted her since that night and she was perfectly fine with that.

It was late November, just before Thanksgiving, and she had this overwhelming feeling that something wasn't right with Tanner.

We haven't spoken in months and he insulted the shit out of me, why should I care? she told herself.

But for days, she couldn't shake the feeling that something was wrong so after almost a week of typing messages and then deleting them, she reached out. Just a simple text saying "Happy Thanksgiving" and hoping he's okay.

Four days later, he responds.

"I just got out of the Veterans Affairs Hospital."

As a former Navy vet, that's where he went for all of his medical attention. Ironically, that also became one of Antoinette's specialties at the State Representatives office that she worked for. She had always had a passion for veterans because her father and brother were both Army vets.

"What happened? Are you okay?" Damn, she hates when her gut is right.

"I was feeling very suicidal, and admitted myself to the psych ward. Have to stay alive for my kids."

Alert! Alert! Red flag. Abort mission! Wish him the best and move on! But she couldn't. November 25, she'll never forget that day. That's the day she always celebrates, each year—with or without him. The day he made it out of the psych ward and lived. Twenty-two veterans a day commit suicide in the United States because of lack of true and compassionate mental health care at the VA hospitals. That and most veteran men, like her father and brother, are too proud to admit when they need help. Twenty-two veterans a day. But not Tanner on this day. He survived as so many others don't.

Chapter 3

University is expensive. Antoinette reluctantly had moved back in with her parents after starting university and was living in their basement. The basement was not finished. It was cold, damp and gross. Her stepdad was nice enough to lay carpet down for her and there was a tiny bathroom in the back corner of it so her lazy ass didn't have to go upstairs to pee. She made it a cave using cabinets and bookshelves for walls. The back door of the house led right to the stairs so if she potentially wanted to sneak some men in and downstairs, she could. Donny and her were over as he had caught feelings and she was not about to be a homewrecker, so she wouldn't be sneaking men down in the basement anytime soon regardless. Or so she thought. Her parents were old school. No boys over and no sleeping in the same bed unless you're married. You could date someone for ten years and they still would not let you sleep in the same room without that legally binding marriage contract. Christian life.

"Admittedly…I plan to have the same rules with my kids should I accidentally have any in the future," she would say whenever she complained about their rules.

After November 25th, Tanner and Antoinette were talking again. There was just something about him she couldn't shake. That and she never actually got to fuck him and she felt like he was too good to pass up. After moving into her parents' and setting the basement up as best as she could, she took a risk and invited Tanner over. To clarify, he is only thirty-four years old. He just looks older from the drugs before and during his Navy days, kids, ex-wife and being a paramedic for fifteen years. He injured his back so badly that he couldn't return to being a medic, hence the dishwasher job at Rushing. So only a twelve-year-and-eight-month difference.... Her dads would have a heart attack.

Antoinette was so incredibly nervous leading up to him coming over. They had made out but that was it and she hadn't seen him in months. She was finally going to fuck his brains out and admittedly, she was pumped. Slut shame her all you want, but she needed this. Antoinette shaved every part of her body, lotioned up, put makeup on, a cute little babydoll lingerie dress with booty shorts, and she was ready. You'd think she was getting ready for her honeymoon as a virgin or something.

She had a brilliant plan for letting Tanner in without her parents noticing. Let the dogs outside to go potty and when the dogs came in, so did Tanner. Clever, right? Her parents had three annoying and yappy little Yorkshire terriers, plus she had her own two: Sugar and Beau. She executed her plan and they both headed straight downstairs. There were a lot of nerves. They both knew what was going down but it's a whole 'nother ballgame when neither of you has the same liquid courage you had at the bar. No face-to-face since summer, just texts and late-night phone calls since November with lots of sexual buildup and anticipation.

Tanner climbs in bed and Antoinette breaks the ice by playing a movie. *Halloweentown.* A Disney Channel classic. This was her test. Every time she dated a guy, she always subjected them to watching this movie. While most of them hated it because it was from the 90s and corny, they did it to get in her pants so it became her standard. Anyone who was going to get in her pants had to watch one of her favorite nostalgic movies of all time. Promiscuous women can still be children at heart.

Five minutes in and they were already kissing each other like it was their last day on earth. She missed his lips so much. She has never let anyone distract her from *Halloweentown* before. Tanner rolls over on top, he is hard through the pants. Antoinette can feel it pressing against her as she spreads her legs, booty shorts still on.

I could quite literally kiss him all night.

When he kisses her, it is so deep and passionate. There's also a lot of biting involved... *Mama likes.* He lifted one hand down the top of her tank top and takes one of her breasts out. Licks the nipple until it's hard and then bites. Hard. She let out a moan and he covered her mouth with his other hand.

"Shhh, baby, your parents are upstairs."

Baby? Who are you calling baby? Shut up, Antoinette. Don't ruin this with your Great Wall of China bullshit.

It's a damn waterfall in her shorts. He takes his time and treats the other breast as equal as the first. Antoinette moves her kisses to his neck. Licks in circles and then sucks. He collapses on top of her in pleasure. *Weak spot found.* They both want it so bad but damn, this foreplay is good. Don't care what any guy tells you, ladies. Foreplay is KEY and you deserve it.

Antoinette unbuttons Tanner's jeans and massages his cock with both of her hands.

"Give it to me," she begs.

"Not yet," he whispers and smiles as he moves down.

He takes off her panties and starts to kiss her cellulite-covered thick thighs. Inching closer and closer to her clit as he kisses. Antoinette is a hot-ass mess at this point. She's never enjoyed head, so she considers telling him to stop so they can just fuck. But the other part of her is saying, *This is a whole new world; let him take you for a spin!* She went with the latter and just in time, because he dived right in. The world literally disappeared as he's licking and suckling down there, holding both of her legs down as she squirms.

Is this what real oral is supposed to feel like? Why didn't I let much older guys give me head from the beginning

She orgasmed in his mouth and her legs started to tremble. It was a complete out-of-body experience, one Antoinette had never had before. Tanner smiled with pride as he climbed back on top of her.

"Oh, we're just getting started," he whispered to her as he kissed her neck.

Goosebumps everywhere. He slipped inside her with such ease and he felt so good. He thrusted, holding one of her legs up and using his free hand to choke her. She hadn't had much experience with choking but she was pretty much his number-one fan now and was willing to let him do anything. She was on a high like she had never been before. He was dripping sweat on her face and Antoinette reveled in it. His eyes never left hers. It was like he was staring right into her soul. She had never had someone watch her so intimately and it was ecstasy.

"Are you going to cum for me again?" he asked while still inside and on top.

What? Again? She had also never experienced that either but she obviously didn't want him to know that. She just responded maybe" with a sly grin. *Play it cool,* she told herself. He clearly took that as a challenge as he repositioned to hit her clit with each thrust.

Shit.

He smiled and those dimples made her so hot and weak for him. At this point, both of their bodies were sweaty and lustful and yet, she didn't feel close enough. Antoinette kept pulling him in closer, wanting to feel more. He felt her body preparing to orgasm again.

"That's it, baby," he said to her.

How the hell did he know? she thought.

Just as she finished that thought, Antoinette exploded all over again and Tanner finished along with her. He rolled over and they both just laid there. Silence other than the intense recovery breathing.

He finally got up to pee and once he came back she said to him, "Are you ready for round two?" Both of them grinning from ear to ear.

———

She was sleeping and rolled over to an empty bed. Clock said 3 A.M., where the hell was he? She grabbed a robe and walked upstairs. He was nowhere to be found. She walked outside, his car was on and he was just sitting inside. Antoinette opened the door and he was passed out with a fifth of Jack Daniels between his legs. This was the fourth night this week... it was getting way out of hand.... She was pissed but decided to be nice. She woke him up and he couldn't even speak. Antoinette helped him walk to their bedroom and undressed him as he was snoring loudly. She was wide awake and didn't want to be near him. She started to walk away so that she could go watch TV but the idea of him choking on his own vomit popped in her head. She walked back and propped him on his side with pillows behind his back so that he couldn't move back. She was pissed but also concerned. What is going on with him?

———

Antoinette woke up in a sweat of terror from that nightmare of her past.... She loathed that years later, *he* still haunted her. In a panic, she looked over to her side and saw Tanner passed out, cuddled up next to her. She took a deep breath and smiled knowing he was next to her. That terror dissipated and she fell back asleep....

Chapter 4

It was now winter in Michigan and Antoinette finished up her final semester of college before law school. She went from barely graduating high school to earning the Dean's List her final semester and graduating with a 3.49 cumulative GPA. She would have had a higher grade point average if *he* hadn't prevented her from going to school that first year. But nevermind that, she was proud. Antoinette opted to walk her graduation ceremony in May instead of December because she had family from Arizona who wanted to come up.

Her mom and stepdad were in Florida for three weeks and she was ready to have Tanner all to herself in that time. She snuck Tanner over three to four nights a week that entire semester while taking five classes, one of them being a graduate class. He was her high. His living situation and kid situation were complicated, all red flags, but he was her drug and she felt like she needed him. The first Friday after her semester ended, they planned a taco night. Antoinette doesn't even like tacos. She avoids everything Mexican related after her past with *him*, but she'd deal with it if it meant her own taco getting eaten later that night (bad pun, but still funny). She got the wine out, lit some candles and waited until he walked in by catching up on her Shonda Rhime TGIT shows.

He walks in and Antoinette hears him talking. He must be on the phone.

Then she gets up and sees two Native American kids in her kitchen. Um, what?

"Hi, I'm Jesse," this adorable little four-year-old brown kid says to her. "And this is my brother, Liam," but he said it like "Wee-am."

Liam just shrugged and nodded. He was eleven and in that moody pre-teen stage. Her heart dropped and her vagina shriveled up like a raisin. There went their romantic sleepover with sex all over the house. She was actually speechless (for once) and looked up to see Tanner staring at her, hands full of grocery bags, grinning in triumph.

Both of his sons were half Native American from his Navy days in New Mexico. They honestly looked nothing like him, their moms' genetics were strong. Much like Antoinette's Cuban genetics dominated her looks. Both dark all around—dark skin, dark eyes and dark hair.

"To render you speechless is surely something that deserves rewarding," he said to her as he laughed and winked.

Still no words came out of Antoinette's mouth. *What in the actual fuck is happening right now?*

Tanner continued to set down all the ingredients for their taco nights on the counter. The kids headed to the living room to watch TV and Antoinette continued to just give him that "what the fuck" look.

"I figured if this is going to go anywhere, I need you to meet my kids now. None of that waiting a year to see if this goes somewhere, because then what if we invest all that time only for my kids to hate you or vice versa?"

Solid point.

To clarify, Antoinette used to want kids back in high school. She wanted seven kids, to be exact, just like in the old TV show *7th Heaven*. That all changed when she took a parenting class in 11th grade. Some high schools give you bags of sugar, that is not good birth control at all.

These robot babies were the worst! The student had to wear a wristband that had to connect to your baby every time it cried to show your teacher that the student wasn't just letting robot baby cry the whole weekend. This little shit of a robot baby would continue crying until you either changed it, fed it or rocked it.

That weekend, Antoinette had to go to the school variety show, her best friend's dance competition and church with that *thing*. The looks she was given were atrocious and she was so exhausted by Monday that she dropped off the baby and then went back home to sleep.

Honestly, it was the best birth control ever. All schools should implement it as a mandatory class because after that, Antoinette wanted zero babies. Her teacher offered extra credit to do it again but her mom instead paid her money NOT to do it.

Antoinette figured she would meet his kids in like a year, or two or never. Not today, not when they were only just kind of dating, not even exclusive. She was panicking and he knew it. Tanner knew it and he loved every second of it.

"I love watching you squirm," he said to her. Then he leaned in closer and whispered, "in bed and out," sending chills down her spine and making her lower area perk back up from the raisin it once was. While that made her want to rip his clothes off, she took his remarks and took it as a challenge.

You think you can make me squirm over some damn little parasites? Challenge accepted. I have five nieces and nephews, kids love me. Let's do this.... Who was she trying to convince, him or herself?

Kids are exhausting. It was well after midnight by the time Liam and Jesse fell asleep. After tacos, they watched *Ant Man* and wore each other out with pillow fights and tickle tortures.

Antoinette lost each match and almost peed herself with laughter. She was smitten with those boys already, they definitely had manners and heart like their father. Tanner was raising very sweet, genuine and funny boys. Antoinette was surprisingly more attached after meeting Liam and Jesse, which made her fear of commitment rise up and cause serious anxiety.

———

Maybe this could work. Dude, she can handle the boys and did great with them. Just because she can handle kids doesn't mean she can handle demons like mine.... I should stay away. For her sake. Leave her alone. She is so young with such a bright future ahead...but man, is she beautiful. Come on, Tanner. Focus. You can do this.... Just hide those demons as long as you can.

The rest of Christmas break went by so fast. They had been pretending to be a little family with her parents gone and having the house to themselves with the boys. Jesse was already attached to Antoinette's hips and cuddling her any time he came over. She loved it but also caught herself worrying about those Great Wall of China walls being punctured by a four-year-old. However, Liam had not warmed up as much. He was very possessive of Tanner and didn't like having to share him. She understood it, though, she was the same way with her dad even to this day at twenty-two.

Liam grew up on a reservation in New Mexico going the first five years of his life not knowing Tanner was his dad. He was the result of a one-night stand while Tanner was stationed there in the Navy. By the time Tanner found out about Liam he was already married to another native woman, who was pregnant with Jesse. Red flag #247 here. Two baby mamas from the same reservation. Antoinette could definitely see the big, flashing red flags waving at her, why was she not listening?

Liam was very reserved due to the lack of a father figure and a hellish mother figure. Even though Tanner had come into his life at age five, he still lived in Michigan while Liam was on

the reservation. Liam just moved up to live with Tanner a few months ago and it was a very rocky road. Liam was used to no rules, no structure, and no discipline (unless his mom was drunk). However, Liam was also used to no love, no support and no affection from his mother as well. Antoinette felt for this kid but had no idea how to help. She was spoiled rotten growing up with two phenomenal biological parents and two great stepparents.

From what Tanner told Antoinette, Liam's mother was an awful woman. According to Liam himself, she was an alcoholic who forced Liam to smoke and drink. If he didn't do as she said, she would kick him out of the house to where he would have to walk to a neighbor's house and sleep on their couch. As much as Antoinette sympathized with Liam, part of her always wondered if maybe he was stretching the truth a bit just to get Tanner to take him in originally. Detective Antoinette couldn't take the case, however, because Liam was going back to New Mexico after the holidays. Apparently he didn't like the structure and wanted to go back to the toxicity that he was used to.

"I don't know how I am going to fly Liam back to New Mexico. I can't afford it," he vented to her in the basement after they had just finished round two.

Five orgasms and counting, he was so generous that Antoinette could barely walk. Her parents were coming back home from Florida in two days and they would have to go back to sneaking around and biting pillows to control her noises.

"Why not drive and take a road trip?" Antoinette asked.

Tanner looked up at her, grinning up to his eyes. What was he looking at her like that? She felt a rock hit her stomach, worried that he was going to make her do something. He knew that he could use his baby-blue eyes and deep dimples to get her to do anything.

"Come with me. We can rent a car, drive across country, fuck on the side of mountains. You can meet my people from when I lived down there, we can make a mini-vacation of it on the way back, just us. Let's do it."

Antoinette almost spit out her coffee at that suggestion. While they had been sleeping together for about a month now, he could still be a murderer. And she worked. And he could be a murderer!

Chapter 5

Welp. They were headed to New Mexico but she only had three days to do it. For reference, the reservation in New Mexico was 1,720 miles away from her home in Southeast Michigan. She had never driven that far. He could dump her body in a ditch and no one would ever find her. She did take the precautions not to end up like Liam Neeson's daughter in *Taken* and shared her location with AJ and her mom. Between having to meet Liam's (not Neeson) grandmother and Tanner's friends from when he lived down there, her stomach was tore up. She was definitely planning on spending the weekend drunk.

You wanna know what you see from Michigan to New Mexico? A whole lot of nothing. Cornfields, plains and absolute nothingness. Antoinette had never visited most of these states and was desperately looking for something fun to do or see on their route. The only thing she could find was the World's Largest Ball of Twine in Cawker City, Kansas. It was about an hour out of the way but she really wanted to show Liam something unique in case she never saw him again.

———

I woke up from a nap to see that Antoinette had taken us off the highway.

MARIAELENA

"Where are we going?" I asked.

I normally never fall asleep when a woman drives, I am surprised I was able to get any rest. She squealed with excitement while she explained to me that we were headed to the World's Largest Ball of Twine. She was so fucking adorable. I'm smiling as I look at her, excited she found something in all this nothingless, when I look down at the fuel gauge. It was on E. This is why I don't let women drive! I asked her when she planned on getting gas and she told me she has been looking for the last hour but hasn't seen anything but cornfields. Then she says, "If we have to pull over and ask some nice farmer to take us to a gas station, it'll be fine. Don't sweat it." Don't sweat it? Woman, we are in the middle of butt-fucking nowhere and the gas tank is on E. I have no idea how many miles until we are actually out but fuck, this is stressful.

We finally find a two-pump gas station deep in some cornfields with no convenience store next to it. Just the pumps. After we filled up, I took the keys and planned to not let her drive again for a long time. Antoinette is cute as hell but I am not getting stranded because of her cuteness.

———

The World's Largest Ball of Twine is just like you would imagine. A massive ball of twine...and probably a waste of gas but it was something none of those three had seen before. Once they reached Clayton, New Mexico, it was time to stop for a night or two. They were staying with one of Tanner's old firefighter buddies who had a house, fiancé and kid. Clayton, New Mexico, is tiny. It has a population of 3,000 people, has one gas station and has two restaurants. Driving into Clayton is all desert with no street-lamps and Antoinette almost hit a coyote driving on the way into town. Once they arrived at the friend's house, they all passed out from driving almost 20 hours straight and decided to start over in the morning.

The next morning, she woke up to Tanner laughing in the kitchen with his buddy, Joe. Joe was a tall, lengthy guy, possibly native too. Very dark skin, hair and eyes. His fiancé was polar opposite with snow-white skin and bright blonde hair. Liam was still passed out on the floor and she was on the couch. She got up and ran to the bathroom to look somewhat presentable. She didn't want to interrupt Tanner and Joe going down memory lane so she sat back down on the couch and decided to check her phone. She had an email. From *him*. She blocked his number that night at the masquerade.

Mamacita. I miss you. I am sober, please give me another chance. Don't make me come find you....

Fuck. She moved. Her parents moved. She changed numbers, jobs, everything. How could he find her?

He can't find you. Calm down. Get up, enjoy your man and relax.

Well, fuck that. She couldn't relax at all. She was in a daze the entire day. Tanner could tell something was up but she didn't want him know about her stupid past so she froze up and made that Great Wall of China extra sturdy. Nighttime finally came where it was socially acceptable to drink and man, did she need it. Antoinette downed shot after shot of Fireball with no chaser. By eight o'clock she was drunk and Tanner was clearly irritated. Antoinette didn't care, commitment isn't her thing and this is why. Ain't no man gonna tell her how to act.

It was now ten o'clock and Antoinette was making a damn fool of herself. Tanner whispered in her ear to follow him to the bedroom. *Absolutely, yes, please,* she thought to herself. He told them he'd be right back, led Antoinette to the room and closed the door behind them. His lips were instantly on hers and she was intoxicated from him and the alcohol.

"I am going to make you orgasm and then you are going to bed and sleeping the liquor off, do you understand me?"

"Two orgasms," she bartered.

"No, ma'am. You haven't been a good girl today. One orgasm and I won't punish you."

"Okay, Daddy," she said to him as he headed straight for her breasts.

In between each kiss and suckle, he told her how frustrating and spoiled she was. It only turned her on more. He pulled her yogas off and stuck two fingers down there, rubbing her clit. Tanner pushed her on the couch and unzipped his pants. Antoinette wanted head but he reminded her that he had friends waiting for him. She was wet with anticipation so once he entered her, the orgasm didn't take long.

"Act like this again in front of my people and next time, you won't get an orgasm," he said to her in a playful warning.

Tanner tucked her in on the couch and kissed her forehead. She was already almost asleep. She was so beautiful, even as a drunken mess.

———

The next morning, she woke up with an excruciating headache and embarrassment to last a lifetime. They went and had breakfast at a small little diner called 87 Restaurant and met up with even more of Tanner's old firefighter buddies. Their table had about sixteen people there and Antoinette was definitely overwhelmed. Apparently green chili is a huge thing down in New Mexico and just the color was enough to turn Antoinette off but seeing Tanner do a little kid dance when his green chili omelet came out made her thankful for that weird green slime.

Everyone said their goodbyes after breakfast and the three amigos headed to the reservation to drop Liam off. To avoid awkward introductions and help prevent Antoinette from throwing up due to anxiety, she requested they do the *exchange* at the nearest McDonald's so that she could hide inside while they caught up outside. Chicken.

Not even two hours into driving back to Michigan and the sexual tension was through the roof between Tanner and Antoinette. She started to unzip his pants and play with him as he drove. Then she unbuckled her seatbelt and let her lips take over from what her hands had been doing. Tanner pulled over at the first exit he saw right onto a construction site. Thankfully, it was well after dark so nobody was there. He shut off the car and grabbed her head as she continued to taste his cock. You could tell how much he loved her lips on his dick with the way he moaned and squirmed.

Tanner then stopped her and climbed over to the passenger seat right on top of her. He undid her pants and she was already wet and ready. He slid right in and instantly knew he wouldn't last long with how good she felt.

"Baby, I am not going to last long. Can you cum for me?" he pleaded.

She shook her head and told him his pleasure was all she needed. He exploded inside her and she smiled. Man, did she love that "O" face.

––––––––

The next twenty-two hours of driving was torture for them. Starting a trip is always fun but the way back, whether plane, train or automobile, seems to take much longer. Both of them reeked from lack of showers but they had to drive straight through because Antoinette worked Monday morning at 11:00 A.M. No time for hotel rooms and no time for showers. By the last ten hours, Antoinette wouldn't even have sex with Tanner because of how self-conscious she was without a shower. At the soonest rest stop they found, Antoinette gave herself a whore bath in an attempt to not feel so grimy but she still was not letting him anywhere near her.

Regardless of the stench, their chemistry was undeniable. Antoinette was driving through Illinois (home stretch) and Tanner was just looking at her with such thirst in his eyes. He devoured her with his eyes, making her blush. She said, "No, I stink!" But he didn't care. His hands started sliding around her thighs, instantly making her lose her breath. Then he started to unbutton her pants wanting so much more of her...while she was driving on a toll highway.

"Don't. We're going to get in a car accident and die," she pleaded.

Tanner still didn't listen and to be honest, she did not really want him to. He stuck his fingers down her pants and behind the panties. She was wet and her words were definitely not matching what her body was saying. He continued playing with her downstairs while he kissed her neck.

One heck of a way to die, I guess.

Antoinette decided to then take charge. She could not drive safely and orgasm but she could please him, which he deserved. She took one free hand and unbuttoned his pants. His dick was already hard and desperate to come out. She told him to grab her lotion in the back seat while still massaging him. When she told him to squeeze a bunch of lotion in her hand, he looked at her in shock, excited shock. That pure joy that came across his face when he realized he was getting an old-fashioned hand job was like when a baby tries ice cream for the first time.

Antoinette took her cock hand and took the time to adjust the rearview mirror on Tanner's face so she could watch him enjoy her hands. Watching him and watching the road was no easy sign. As she looks up to watch the road, she sees a sign:

TOLL BOOTH: 3 MILES

Shit.

"You've got three minutes or less to cum. We're about to hit a toll."

Challenge accepted and mission accomplished.

————

They were in Michigan heading east only five hours away. A massive snowstorm hit and the great lake effect made the drive awful. They couldn't possibly go another minute without resting their eyes so they pulled over at another small rest stop for a nap. They both passed out within minutes. Within an hour, Antoinette woke up to Tanner talking but when she opened her eyes, she realized he was still asleep. He was shaking and started screaming, "No, no, leave her alone!" Concerned, she shook him to wake him up and he almost knocked her lights out in the process. Antoinette was terrified. Red Flag #304.

"Why did you wake me up?" he demanded, screaming at her.

After she explained why she woke him, Tanner got out of the car and took a walk to cool off...in the snowstorm. What was his deal? He was having a nightmare clearly and Antoinette was helping him out. She had never seen him go so crazy and it made her stomach upset. He finally got back in the car and looked at her with such somber eyes.

"Do you believe in Native American spirits?" he asked.

"Like dead people or voodoo?"

"Yes."

"No...," she said quizzingly. *He lost his damn marbles. Voodoo isn't real and his ex-wife's people can't get him in his sleep....*

They spent the rest of the car ride back home in silence. Once they arrived, Antoinette had to go straight back to work with no shower. She was on maybe three hours of sleep, three days without a shower and cranky because she felt Tanner went psycho on her without any explanation other than some sort of spirits were trying to haunt him. What a fun day at work this was going to be.

Chapter 6

With Liam gone, Tanner and Antoinette had so much extra time together…which meant extra sexy time as well. After their road trip to New
Mexico and back, they had decided to become *exclusive*. Antoinette's parents were not pleased; a thirteen-year age gap with two kids and a di-
vorce was a lot for them to process and accept. She didn't care, Tanner
was unlike any man she had ever met. She would leave for work in the
morning and there would be a single

rose or teddy bear on her car that Tanner had left in the middle of the
night while she was sleeping. He would bring her favorite coffee drink
to work or spend her lunch break with her. He would write her notes
and love letters and leave them around for her to find randomly.

He had even taken the time to buy her an engraved leatherbound Bible
with thick pages to highlight and red lettering for when Jesus spoke just
like the one her grandmother had that passed away when she was ten
years old. She had only mentioned that once during one of their phone
conversations at 4 A.M. and somehow he had made it happen and re-
membered every little detail. He was the most giving (in bed and out),
genuine and loving man she had ever met.

It was a slow Monday at work and Antoinette was bored of her mind at the office. Tanner surprised her with her favorite French vanilla coffee like he had done many times before but this time, he added a twist. Antoinette's boss and coworker were out of town so she locked the door and stopped pretending to work as soon as he arrived. While giving Tanner the unofficial tour of the small office heading for the couch with a make-out session in her mind, he threw in another twist by turning around and kissing her. Hard. That kiss was all she needed to know to realize what he wanted and it was not just a make-out session. Antoinette warned him that she was on her period as she was unsure how he felt and he only leaned up closer, pressing his hard dick through his pants against her.

"I have never had sex on a desk before...let alone that of a State Representative," he said to her with wanting eyes.

She had never cleared her boss's desk so quickly.

———

Antoinette really wanted Tanner to meet her Cuban family down in Arizona. Her father and aunt came over to the United States from Cuba under Fidel Castro's communist rule as children. Once Fidel took power over the country, he gave citizens two years to leave and fortunately, thousands of them did. Antoinette's grandfather tried keeping their family in Cuba because he was a communist but her grandmother was able to leave and create a new life for them. Antoinette was proud of her heritage and her family for all the sacrifices they made to come to this country. Plus she gets her curves and sass from that Cuban side.

Her father served in the Army once he graduated high school and was in the special forces until he was honorably discharged because his first wife was pregnant with her now older brother (who was ironically only two years older than Tanner). Her dad being a veteran was just another reason she was drawn to Tanner. He could be a scary dude when he wanted to be at 6 '4", 230 lbs., but he was also the most loving, caring, and gentle (in his older age) man she knew. No man could compare to him.

Antoinette decided to book a short trip to Arizona with Tanner and let the Cubans at him. This was their first real trip together, real vacation. She also booked a small mini-cruise as a surprise; she loved spoiling him.

––––––––––

Everything was going wonderfully. Her family, while hesitant about the age difference and baggage, loved Tanner. Tanner knew how to swoon everyone he met with his charisma and genuine demeanor. He could bond to just about anybody and connect with them. He connected with her father on past military life. He connected with her brother on ex-wives, custody fights, previous addictions, and military life (Red Flag #478). He connected with her tia ("aunt" in Spanish) on spirituality and being a Christian. He connected with everyone and it only made Antoinette love him more.

One morning after Cuban bread and cafe con leche for breakfast, her tia and dad had left to pick up some groceries, leaving just Tanner, Antoinette and her tio (uncle), who was watching TV. When Antoinette's tio watched TV, a burglar could come in the house and steal shit and he wouldn't even realize it with how focused he became. They were basically all alone in the house and she knew exactly what she wanted to do. Sleeping in separate beds for the last two nights since coming back from the cruise because her family were strict Christians was really making her horny.

Tanner was in the bathroom peeing when Antoinette walked in.

"Can I help you with something?" he sarcastically asks while she's watching him finish up.

"Sit down," she orders him as she pushes the toilet seat shut.

He does so and she locks the door.

Antoinette kneels down and slowly lowers his boxers and pants while he stays seated.

"Babe, no, your tio is right in the living room."

She ignores his objection and starts massaging him to get him hard, staring directly in his eyes. Once it's pretty hard, she puts her mouth over it and begins massaging with her mouth. Tanner stops her, grabs her by the ponytail and pulls her to her feet, slowly taking off her shorts and then her panties. She is already wet, he does not need to help her get there. Antoinette climbs on top and straddles Tanner while he stays seated on the toilet, his cock slides right in. God, he feels glorious. She could cum instantly and he knows it.

"No, baby. Not yet," he pleads with her in a whisper.

She continues riding his dick, he's massaging her breasts. He kisses her and the world escapes. They're no longer hiding in her aunt's bathroom on a toilet seat, they are floating. Antoinette and Tanner move their hips in unison like synchronized swimmers, his hands on her ass and lips on her neck. She can't hold it any longer as she orgasms all over his dick. Tanner grins and sticks his fingers down there and then licks them just so he can taste her. He bends her over the sink to see that glorious glow-in-the-dark ass and finishes inside of her. Wrapping up their visit to Arizona on a great endnote.

———

"I'm joining a motorcycle club," Tanner says to her randomly while they're eating tacos.

He could tell by her expression that she was not on board.

"I've always wanted to join one," he continued, "and this won't be like the ones you see on TV where they sell drugs and beat up people. This will just be a place of camaraderie for me. I'll have my boys and you can be my 'old lady.' I'd like you to come with me to meet the vice president of a club I'm looking at. We'll just have a few beers, chat and see what you think and how it goes. What do you say?"

Camaraderie? Who needs camaraderie when you have me?

"Okay." That's all she said in response.

Tanner knew she wasn't thrilled with the idea, he could feel the tension in the room. Y'all ever watched *Sons of Anarchy*? Yes, Jax Teller is a beautiful man and who doesn't appreciate his perfectly defined ass in those sex scenes. But holy fuck. The drugs, the violence, prostitution, murder! That was all Antoinette could think about every time Tanner mentioned a motorcycle club.

A few days later, they met up with Rex, Vice President for Black Rebel Motorcycle Club. Tanner had to meet with Rex before meeting the big man in charge, and president of the MC, Phil. *What kind of name is Rex?* Antoinette's claws were out and her walls up tonight. *Why does he need camaraderie? Why am I not good enough? Why couldn't he just have like one or two guy friends?* She had all these questions (really, insecurities of not being enough) that slowly chipped away at her confidence and trust in him which, let's face it, was her problem and she had no right getting salty.

But she hated motorcycles, always had, and that was the perfect excuse to not be on board...right?

Tanner and Antoinette walk into this empty-ass bar on a Monday night with only three people scattered around. Antoinette planned on getting drunk and ordered two martinis to start. Rex began to explain what the MC stood for and what they looked for in a member. She had no clue why it bugged her so much but she was mad. These red flags aren't all Tanners. She didn't want this and she was the queen of control freaks. How else do you think she kicked ass academically and professionally? Her biggest problem was she didn't know where to stop controlling....

Antoinette had become pretty tipsy pretty fast. Her words were slurring and she was being a straight-up bitch to Rex, questioning everything about him and this MC he represented. He was giving her shit back, though, which impressed her. Rex was half Mexican, which took their competition of who can give more shit to another level. Level Cuban v Mexican. Antoinette hated most Mexicans, though. Something about them gave her PTSD due to *him*.

In the middle of their bullshitting, Tanner got up and walked out...for a smoke, she thought, but then he never came back.

"Where did you go?" she texted him.

"I left."

"Um, why? How am I supposed to get home?"

"I left the car and started walking. I figured you and Rex were having such a good time, you didn't need me."

"What in the actual fuck are you talking about?" She was puzzled and on her fifth martini. Or was it her sixth? It was too many at this point, especially to be driving anywhere.

Tanner continued, "I know you like him. You are picking on him and giving him shit because you like him. That's how you treated me at *Rushing* before we started hooking up. You like him and are flirting. I'm not going to stand by and watch you two flirt. I'm done, I'm out."

At this point, Antoinette is fuming and Rex is asking where Tanner went. She didn't want to tell him what Tanner was accusing them of and ruin his chances of getting into this stupid MC. She didn't find Rex remotely attractive in the slightest but was a natural flirt and maybe she had been flirting without realizing it? She played it cool and told him she was running outside to grab Tanner.

She headed outside and as soon as she got to the parking lot, she saw him sitting down on the curb, scrolling on his phone.

"What the hell are you doing? Get your ass back in there, you look like an idiot."

The martinis were not sugarcoating anything tonight. Shit, she never sugarcoated anything anyways, martinis or not. Sugarcoating is for defense attorneys, not prosecutors.

"I look like a damn idiot because you're flirting with a man whose club I want to join!"

"I am not flirting with him, stupid! I have eyes for you and only you!"

There was pure rage and hurt in his eyes. *Why was he so self-conscious? I tell him how handsome and beautiful he was daily, if not multiple times a day. There was no one else on this planet I wanted more.*

After ten minutes of Tanner yelling at Antoinette and her begging him to go back inside and quit blowing his shot, he finally agreed. While he did agree to go back inside, he didn't necessarily believe that she wasn't flirting with Rex. Her buzz had worn off and she didn't speak the rest of the night. *Since when do you cower to a man, Antoinette?* She hated herself. She was an independent boss bitch who didn't need no man. She hadn't been this upset with herself in years.

"You stupid whore! I saw you flirting with that bus boy!" he screamed at her in a drunken rage.

He couldn't even stand straight. They were in his parents' basement and she kept begging him to stay quiet so they wouldn't come down and see what was going on. Why SHE was begging him in HIS parents' house while he was screaming at her made absolutely no sense, looking back.

"Baby, I wasn't flirting with him. I was just talking to him. You flirt with servers in the kitchen all the time!"

He corners her against a wall, grabbing her arms so hard, she can't move. His breath reeked of Jack Daniels.

"You're a liar. It slowed down and I headed to the host stand to say hi to you and what do I see? You're flirting with that bus boy!"

SLAP. Right across her face. Tears started falling down her face. It hurt but he didn't do it as hard as he wanted; he knew how to not leave marks.

The more she argued and swore to him that she didn't, the harder he squeezed her arms. She knew how to diffuse him—this had happened so many times. She cried and apolo-

gized for something she didn't do. As soon as he saw the tears and heard her apologize, he lightened his grip.

He dragged her to the bed and sat her down. Kissing her neck and apologizing for being rough. He just needed to remind her that she cannot look at anyone else. She belongs to him, he told her. She swallowed her tears and fear, agreed to every word and let him climb on top and inside of her as she pretended she was on a beach elsewhere....

———

Antoinette woke up in a sweat from that memory surfacing into a nightmare. Why was she still dreaming of *him?* That was years ago. And he didn't know where she lived anymore, he couldn't hurt her...right?

———

April showers brought May flowers this year for sure. Tanner ended up with some serious medical issues and was in and out of the hospital for weeks. He went to the Veterans Affairs Hospital in Ann Arbor for severe anal pain. They turned out to be anal fissures, which were basically like taking a razorblade to your asshole. Antoinette snuck out of work early or took extra-long lunch breaks every day he was there. She stayed the night in the hospital, brought him food, helped him shower and yelled at the nurses to make sure he was receiving the best care. Full-on wifey mode.

"I know you really like this guy but you've only been dating a few months and look at all the issues he's having. He's much older than you with a lot of baggage, are you sure he's worth it?" her coworker asked.

The audacity.

His head game alone is worth this. Does that make her a slut? *A slut with too many orgasms to count,* she grinned. She was going crazy having a full-ass conversation in her head while her coworker looked at her concerned. Antoinette ignored the anger festering inside of her and she politely explained why he was worth it to her.

Tanner was finally discharged after two weeks and he was so drugged up on painkillers that he slept most of the day. Antoinette took it upon herself to go to the grocery store and get him food—liquids only. Jell-O, soup, pudding, ice cream.

Who am I? This gross, lovestruck, domesticated puppy. What about Washington? What about being president? He isn't leaving his kids....

DING.

Ope, maybe it's Tanner!

"Hey, Sexi Cubi."

Instant nausea. She knew exactly who it was.

DING.

"You can't ignore me forever. We are soulmates, mi amor."

Antoinette starts to panic. She goes into the bathroom at Kroger to calm down. Does she reply and tell him to fuck off like she had multiple times? *No. Just block this new number, now.*

DING.

"I am back in Michigan, mi amor. I will find you and make this right. Xxoo."

Blocked.

———

It's 10 A.M. on a Monday and Antoinette gets a text from Tanner's best friend, Hope. Yes, his best friend is a female but her best friend is of the opposite sex also. You can be friends with the opposite sex and not cross lines, y'all. Proof is in the pudding. Hope is a tall, skinny beanpole with crazy, curly hair. She is married to an equally tall, skinny beanpole, but they have two Michelin Man babies. Genetics are confusing.

"Hey, don't panic but I just called an ambulance for Tanner. He blacked out while we were on the phone. They're taking him to the University of Michigan this time since the VA ain't shit."

True.

In less than 60 seconds, Antoinette was out the door and in her car, on the way to the hospital.

How could he have blacked out? Why did he black out? What if something worse is going on? Hope said not to panic but full-panic mode was engaged and there was no stopping it.

Antoinette walked into the emergency room entrance to find him lying in a bed with his mom next to him. *First, he hates his mom, so why is she here? Secondly, what thirty-something-year-old man has their mom come to the hospital with him? Rude, Antoinette. You would want your mom here too, ya jackass.*

———

A week later, he was discharged again. The VA really ain't shit because U of M fixed him up in a week when two weeks at the VA only made him worse. It wasn't totally their fault. They are severely understaffed and don't pay the best wages so they get shit people half the time.

Antoinette couldn't imagine vets who fought for this country getting treated how Tanner was and not having a crazy, aggressive girlfriend to stand up for them.

"I don't want to deal with anybody but you tonight. Let's get a room," Tanner suggested in his weakened and pathetically adorable voice. He can barely walk, he is in so much pain, but of course she loves the idea of getting a hotel room.

Antoinette starts a hot bath for him and helps him in. This is intimacy and she lived for it. The closeness, the trust. As if he was reading her mind, he said, "I want to say I love you but I think it's too soon." Her heart sank. God, he was beautiful.

She smiled back at him while they laid there in the warm water together and said, "I want to say I love you too but it is definitely too soon."

Was it, though? Was it too soon to drive across the country and back in a short week-end? Was it too soon to spend your nights in the hospital being by his side? We've already been through so much…you know how you feel.

They hadn't had sex since his first hospital trip and Antoinette was craving his touch. It had been weeks, almost a month. However, she wasn't going to pressure him with all the pain he was in but there it was again, the one mind. He knew exactly what she was thinking and wanting. After the bath, they were lying in bed with the sexual tension rising. That wasn't the only thing rising. Antoinette's triple-D tits were rising and falling with his eyes, nipples hard with anticipation. Before she could object and tell him to rest, his weak ass was on top of her, kissing her…thanking her. His kisses took her to another planet. When he kissed her, the rest of the world literally escaped.

But there was something different with these post-hospital kisses. They weren't hard and full of lust as they had always been. They were gentle and sweet, which was weird and yet wonderful. This was their first time making love instead of just sex. *Yes, corny but real.* Everything was in slow motion and it felt like the bed was literally floating in the air. When he entered her, she lost her breath. Their two bodies became one, moving so sensually. Antoinette could tell he was in pain but he told her that she felt worth that pain. She exploded all over his cock and quivered beneath him. He followed her lead and then they both fell asleep in each other's arms until the following morning. They knew it then that they loved each other but social norms prevented them from saying it.

Chapter 7

It was now the end of summer and there was no denying they were madly, deeply and hopelessly in love. They were official in every way and the world knew it. They spent every waking moment together that they could with Jesse and without. Antoinette was madly in love with this little boy. He had stolen her heart so deeply and she wanted to spend the rest of her life watching him grow and become a man. Jesse was a part of her now, whether or not Tanner and her worked out.

She was starting law school, had this delicious sex god of a boyfriend and worked full time helping veterans and immigrants for her job. She hadn't heard from *him* since that grocery store incident months prior and was confident she had been ridden of *him* for good. She was the happiest she had ever been and was in love with her life.

"Babe, I am so nervous. It is my first day and I'm going to puke!" she said to Tanner as she sat in the parking lot of her new law school waiting to go inside. She worked till 5 P.M. every day and then drove to Detroit to attend University of Detroit Mercy Law School class 6-9 Monday through Thursday. She was a beast. Antoinette had received a 75% scholarship at Detroit Mercy, which made it easy for her to make them her top choice, and she was so grateful for that scholarship. Her hard work in undergrad definitely paid off.

"Just don't trip and fall," he responded.

That was all he said to her on her first day and it was perfect for her because it made her smile and forget the anxiety...just for a split second. She was wearing a black suit dress and her red heels. She had to make a great first impression. Her red lipstick and bright Jessica Rabbit red hair matched the heels perfectly and she looked incredible. She said goodbye to her man and walked into her very first law school class: Civil Procedure.

Tanner came over after that brain-draining class to show her how proud he was of her. His present? Not the normal two orgasms but three. *Older men are everything.*

"I have something I need to ask you...tell you."

Great, what is it now?

"Jesse's birthday is coming up and we, his mom and I, would like to do a joint birthday party. We want to show him that just because we aren't married anymore doesn't mean we aren't a family...and that includes you. And her new boyfriend, Braden. I understand if you aren't comfortable yet but Jesse loves you and would be sad if you weren't there. No pressure, though."

No pressure? How was there no pressure when you used the almost-five-year-old that I adore against me? Ugh, and look at those dimples. And his baby blues. I could be friends with her, right? I mean, they're divorced. Why couldn't we be friends...?

Antoinette grew up in a blended family as well. Her parents divorced before she turned one and were both remarried by the time she was seven years old. She was raised with four parents and wouldn't have wanted it any other way, honestly. *He* always said that if they got married and had kids, they'd have to stay together forever, even if they were miserable, "for the kids." She never understood that. She was raised with seeing both sets of parents happy and in love, who wouldn't want their parents happy? Neither of her parents ever spoke ill of each other her entire life and if her dad hadn't lived 2,000 miles away, she would've been raised the way Jesse is being raised: all four parents at birthday parties. If she was going to be with Tanner the rest of her life, she would want to model after her parents and put Jesse first.

Antoinette obviously had to go to this birthday party. Jesse was a huge chunk of her heart now and she loved that boy immensely. She invited her other brother, who had two equally aged kids, as a buffer; she needed her own people in case shit hit the fan. She tried to stay busy the entire time by setting up tables, doing goodie bags, bossing servers around and making sure everyone was having fun. Everyone but herself to avoid Jesse's mom or watching Tanner and her like a creep. Yes, she *wanted* to aim to be like her parents but it still hadn't been a year and she had a very large possessive trait.

"Why aren't you with your honey?" her brother asked.

"Um, because he's with his ex-honey and their kid and I feel weird," she responded.

"Don't," he said, "you are way prettier than her. It looks like she got hit in the face with a frying pan. Her face is super flat and eyes are too big for her face."

Leave it to my brother to build me up by tearing someone else down.

Their relationship was never good until he had kids. He was eight years older than her and spent most of his young adult life doing drugs and hanging out with the wrong people. Surprisingly, Antoinette was the good kid out of the two of them but having kids really turned him around and for the better. Now they were very close and those two kids of his were her world.

It was time for cake and the segregation was really starting to be noticeable. Jesse was sitting right between his parents, as he should be, but then his mom's friends and Tanner's family swarmed the rest of the table, leaving Antoinette alone with her brother and his kids so far from the action that they couldn't see a cake. Not his presents, not his cake, nothing. Antoinette fought back tears and the desire to leave. Tanner didn't even notice that she was a football field away or how uncomfortable she was. She had so many questions and as time passed without Tanner noticing, the angrier she got.

Antoinette's mother remarried her first husband, now her stepdad, after they had been separated for almost nine years. During that nine years, her mom married her biological dad and had her. The time apart apparently helped her first husband, and brother's biological dad, heal and become a better man. Her mom went right back to husband #1 immediately after divorcing her biological father. Some would even hint that she might have been double dipping.

What if all Tanner needs is some time apart from me to "heal and become a better man"? What if we spend years apart and then end up back together stronger than ever like my mom and stepdad? Good Lord, what did I get myself into?

After the party, Tanner's ex-wife takes Jesse home and they have a date night. Antoinette was still unsure and trying to convince herself that maybe she was overreacting. After dinner downtown, Tanner took the car and headed toward the horse tracks instead of heading him. *Rendezvous in the car?*

He climbs over to the other side and kisses her.

"Thank you for today. You are a rockstar non-stepmom."

She begins to unbutton his pants and he turns her around in the front seat to see her beautiful glow-in-the-dark ass. Before he sticks his throbbing-hard dick in her, he gets her nice and wet with his fingers. Antoinette had never come before from fingers but she knew with Tanner, anything was possible. She was wet and aching for him; she backed her ass into his groin, begging for it. When he slid in and the world escaped around them. They completely forgot they were cramped in the front seat of a car in the downtown parking lot. Thank God for tinted windows.

Tanner is going hard and deep, slapping her ass and pulling her hair while she bites down on her arm to try and muffle the sound of her screams. The windows are fogged up and the car is most definitely shaking. Anyone walking by knew what was going on. Just when Antoinette thinks Tanner is about to finish, he pulls out. Before she can ask why, his hands are spreading her ass cheeks and his tongue is on her asshole.

WHAT IN THE ACTUAL FUCK IS GOING ON. I am freaky, I really am but the asshole has always kind of been off limits for me. Mama always raised me that this was an exit only.

He started to finger her while he continued licking. She didn't hate it but she also didn't enjoy it. Once he *finished* doing what he was doing to her asshole, he slid deep back inside her and didn't stop until he exploded all over her ass. Antoinette planned to not kiss him for at least two days!

They were getting Chinese food and he was noticeably drunk. He forced her to drive him here or said he would drive to the buffet himself. He could barely walk, she had to hold all his plates for him.

"Oye, amigo," he said to his friend behind the sushi line.

Antoinette wondered why a Mexican was making sushi at a Chinese restaurant. The friend could read her and tell she was uncomfortable but thankfully he acted normal. They just talked in Spanish while she sat there quietly like a good little girl. After he ate his food and tried to steal the salt shaker, she had finally convinced his drunk ass to go home. The entire car ride home he blamed her for his dinner being cut short and for not being "fun." It was a Wednesday afternoon, who gets that belligerent on a Wednesday afternoon alone? She stayed silent as she always did when he was like this. She knew that fighting back or defending herself when he was like this would only make him angrier.

As they pulled up, he got out of the car and ran to open it up for her. Trying to apologize after losing his cool, that was normal. As he helps her out, he begins to kiss her and lift her dress up. Broad daylight in the summer with kids playing outside. She said no and suggested they go inside. Round two of his anger. Why hasn't his buzz worn off yet, she wondered. He's screaming at her and blaming her for his drinking problem. Antoinette says, "I'll see you tomorrow. I can't do this right now," through her tears. She gets in the car and he slams the car door on her leg before she can get it inside. She heard a crack and the tears turned into waterfalls.

He walked away and she drove home with the wrong foot while her normal driving foot was swollen, bruised and possibly fractured knowing that he'll apologize once he's slept it off and she'll pretend it doesn't hurt that bad....

Chapter 8

Antoinette's dog, Sugar, died shortly after little Jesse's 5th birthday in late September and she lost sight of things after that. She started failing her law school classes and didn't care to put in the effort. Some may think it is silly because "a dog is just a dog" but Antoinette had never been like that. Her pets were her life. They were her children and she loved them so deeply that even she didn't understand the bond. She spent at least 30% of her income making sure her pets had the best top-grade food, phenomenal vet and healthcare, and were spoiled rotten.

Sugar toward the end couldn't see, which made walking difficult. She also lost her appetite and forgot to eat so Antoinette would microwave expensive wet dog food and spoon feed it to Sugar just to get her to eat. She had had Sugar on and off since she was ten years old. The last three years were the best for both of them because it created a very deep and loving bond. When Sugar died, Antoinette's world shattered. Tanner was there every step of the way with no judgment and just love.

The day Sugar died, Tanner found a transformation photo of Antoinette and Sugar that had one of them when Antoinette was ten and another one of them when Antoinette was 23 and he printed it on a large easel for her. It only made her cry more when he gave it to her but it was something that she would keep her entire life. Antoinette continued to self-sabotage her life for weeks after Sugar died. She was drinking wine every night after school and liquor every weekend. She had also gotten back into her old habit of chain-smoking cigarettes. She was an absolute wreck.

Tanner was determined to help her or at least distract her. The big University of Michigan v. Ohio State football game was coming up and he dragged her out of the house to watch it at a dive bar. They loved dive bars. He rented a hotel room that night right next to the dive bar so they could walk if needed to. They sat right at the bar dressed in maize and blue to support their team and drank their hearts out. She had never dated someone who loves watching Michigan football as much and it was one of the things that just brought them closer together. When they weren't at a bar drinking and watching the game, they were at her parents' house watching it with Jesse, teaching him the passion too.

Yelling at the TV during the game helped Antoinette from crying. By half-time, they were seeing double from all the alcohol and the sexual tension was too high to wait another two periods for release.

"Let's walk to the hotel room, I will make you cum for Daddy, and then head back for the second half during the halftime show," Tanner said to her with those delicious dimples and baby-blue eyes.

Before she could answer, which would've been an obvious yes, he was grabbing her jacket and pulling her out the door.

The hotel they booked wasn't five-star by any means but it was clean and by the bar so they were happy. The only room they had available was a double with two beds. As soon as the elevator doors shut, he was devouring her lips drunkenly as if he couldn't breathe without them. His hands were already up her shirt when *DING*, the doors opened. They practically ran for the room so hungry for each other and slammed the door shut.

Antoinette began to rip his clothes off and kiss his neck. She loved when she devoured his neck and he turned into putty in her hands. Tanner pushed her up against a wall and gently choked her while he stole more kisses. It was like in those movies where everything is so intoxicating but a complete blur. Drunk sex, borderline incoherent sex, was phenomenal. Their sex was already groundbreaking but add some liquor and it was an out-of-body experience.

He laid her on the bed and ripped Antoinette's pants off, he was already naked and hard for her. He dove deep into her with his tongue and gave so generously as always. Her favorite part of the hotel room was being as loud as they wanted, unlike their secret sexcapades in her parents' basement. Tanner had taken the time over these last months to make her more comfortable with her sexuality and encouraged her to make whatever noises she wanted and as loud as she wanted.

He would never let her make noise back then but Tanner was different. Tanner encourages the noise and gets more turned on with each moan she lets out. He is heating her clit like it's candy and she is begging him to enter her with his cock but he simply refuses with the simple command "Not until you cum in my mouth, baby. I want to taste you." With that, she screams with a deep, intoxicating release in his mouth, and he smiles as he licks her up.

Antoinette is lying there dead as Tanner starts to slowly climb up her stomach with kisses, he is not done with her yet. He reaches her hips, then her belly button before reaching her breasts. So slow and so generous. He takes her tits out of her bra and nibbles at his pleasure. Tanner's tip is right at her clit as he teases her. Antoinette can't take it anymore and grabs his dick to stick it in but he stops her and pulls away.

"Tisk-tisk, baby. Daddy isn't ready yet and now you must wait longer," he says to her as she cries in anticipation and pleads.

He finally enters his deliciously hard dick inside of her and she is so tight and wet. Their rhythm is that of synchronized swimmers, they are one and their motion is unbeatable. She explodes on him again. Her legs are shaking and she's not sure she can handle much more. Not to mention each orgasm takes a toll on her buzz, but he's just getting started.

Tanner takes her legs and pulls them over his shoulders, allowing for full penetration and deep access. Her legs in the air on his shoulders, his hands on her breasts holding up his body weight. Man, she is fucking beautiful. He is thrusting deep in herself, harder and faster with each pump, when all of a sudden he stops.

"What are you doing? Why did you stop?" Antoinette is panting and confused.

"I have to pee...," he drunkenly tells her.

They both start laughing. She expects him to get up to go pee but he just continues lying on top of her thinking.

"Are you going to go?" she asked.

"Can I pee on you?" he asks.

What? Can you pee on me? I guess we do have two beds and I can always shower. Antoinette is contemplating. What the hell, why not? People drink pee when they're stranded in the wilderness, don't they?

Antoinette decides to *Hakuna Matata* and let Tanner do his thing. He starts to rub his hard dick near her lower lips and a little bit of pee trickles out. Antoinette is surprisingly turned on, which scares her even more.

"Pee inside of me," she whispers to him.

Alcohol makes you do weird things.

Tanner pees a bit more on her and then slides himself into her and starts to thrust. He double checks with her to make sure if she is sure and with her smile of confirmation, he lets it rip and empties his bladder while inside of her. She is having the same reaction as you are right now at this very moment. Horror and shock.

She doesn't feel anything during that but pretends to enjoy it because Tanner is very turned on by it. Shortly after he finishes doing *that*, and his body starts to tense, he is ready to cum.

"Can you cum for me a third time, baby?" he pleads with such hope in his voice.

Three times, she is fucking spoiled but she says, "Hell yes."

He looks in her eyes and knows what he needs to do for her to cum with him. Tanner leans in closer and kisses her while thrusting with that perfect rhythm. They're both ready. He puts one hand over her throat and another on her ass. Soaking wet from sweat (and pee), they both explode together, reaching a whole new ecstasy.

Well, that was new. I need a damn shower.

They went back to the bar after changing into new clothes, pretty much sober from all the orgasms, and soon realized there was only seven minutes left in the Michigan football game.

How long was our damn sexcapade?!

———

The following weekend Antoinette was at it again. She still hadn't quit drinking after losing Sugar and wasn't sure how much longer Tanner would put up with her bullshit—wasn't sure she cared either. They planned a date to go to a small little restaurant downtown that was having special pumpkin martinis. When it came to pumpkin, Antoinette was as "basic white girl" as it got.

The restaurant was packed when they arrived so they sat at the bar while they waited for a table. Antoinette was wearing black leggings that emphasized her thick thighs and JLo booty with brown riding boots and a lowcut red top to emphasize her other features. Tanner was wearing dark jeans, black shoes and a pink button-up. Real men wear pink. Antoinette was never on board with the pink until Tanner started wearing it. He could wear a potato sack and she would still think he was the most gorgeous man on the planet.

Her first pumpkin martini came and went in less than two minutes so she ordered a second one. Once they were seated and the server came for a drink order, Antoinette ordered her third martini. While looking at the menu, Tanner got out of his chair and hugged an old man with a bald head and beard. Antoinette was tipsy and instantly annoyed, who was this ruining their date night?

With the older man was a younger-looking guy, she guessed his son. He was tall and slender with a beard also and brown curly beard. Tanner walked the two guys over and apparently had invited them to join their date without consulting her. Definitely irritated now. This was definitely a setup. It was Phil, president of Black Rebel MC, and his son, Joe. Apparently, Tanner had passed the meeting with Rex a few weeks prior so this was the next step. *How convenient.*

Next thing she knows it's 11 o'clock at night and she has had at least eight pumpkin martinis. Antoinette has no idea what has been discussed these last three hours but she is so drunk she can barely keep her eyes open. *Did we even eat? Did I black out but stay awake this entire time? Did I just jump through a space-time continuum?*

Antoinette gets up to break the seal and somehow her boots are off. She doesn't know how they're off nor does she care enough to put them on; she walks to the bathroom without shoes. Tanner follows her to the bathroom and she assumes it's for a quickie. She sits down to pee and she smiles at him, asking about the potential quickie with her eyes.

"Absolutely not. I am so pissed off at you," he says, and he looks pissed.

She is actually seeing two of him and both versions look pissed.

"What did I do?" she asks.

"Why is it every time I am with members of this club, you get wasted and act like a total ass? How old are you? You're embarrassing me!"

Antoinette literally does not remember a damn thing. She couldn't remember the last three hours or what she did but she didn't give two fucks. Her dog died and she didn't care about anyone or anything. Fuck him and his stupid biker gang. She told him that too.

"Okay, well, we are leaving so hold yourself together while I close out our tab," he orders her.

The two MC guys are silent, they can feel the tension between them two. The server comes and drops down martini #9. *Um, when did I order this? Damn it.* Now she is totally and completely aware of just how drunk she is. Tanner asks for the check and tells her to put on her damn boots. They say goodbye to Beard 1 and 2, walk out, and he screams at her the entire way to the car.

Antoinette is balling her eyes out, so confused and at a complete loss of words (and memory). What she wouldn't give for a camera of what she apparently had done or said. They drive to his car, he gets out and slams the door shut. *Fuck you then.* She is so drunk (and aware of it) that she couldn't possibly drive so she crawls into the back seat to take a cap. Tanner knocks on her window so he can drive her home but her pride doesn't allow it. Of course, he still cares about her safety even after she fucks up. Eventually, he gave up and she passed the hell out in the car.

She woke up in her back seat at 3:00 A.M., freezing her ass off with all the windows fogged up. She had twelve missed calls and seven texts all from tanner. Half of them spewing hate for a ruined night but the rest showing concern for her safety. She crawls her less-drunk ass into the driver's seat and drives home without responding to any of the messages.

Once she got home safely, she headed straight for the toilet and puked up nine pumpkin martinis. She swore that night to never have anything pumpkin flavored again.

Chapter 9

You would think that after the pumpkin martinis, Tanner would have left her ass. She needed therapy in all honesty, they both did. But nope, they did the complete opposite and decided to move in together. Everything at her parents' house reminded her of Sugar and she wanted to start over. Plus think about all the monumental sex they could have 24/7 living together.

They, mainly Antoinette, picked a cute two-bedroom, two-full-bath apartment. It had beige carpeting everywhere except for the living room and bathrooms. The sliding door went right out to the patio and grass so it would be easier for her to let out her other dog, Beau.

Within the first two days, Antoinette had it looking like a home with pictures and dollar store decor everywhere. Tanner thought it was weird but she ignored it. She needed pictures in order for it to feel like a home to her, she had always been like that.

The first bedroom was theirs complete with a new black bed frame for the king mattress and matching black nightstands. She then decked out the second bedroom for the boys, mainly Jesse but also for Liam if he ever came back to Michigan. Antoinette bought a brand-new bunkbed with a twin on top and full-size mattress on the bottom. Top bunk had a Spiderman sheet set for Jesse and a lime green with black for Liam on the bottom. She sat the bunkbed right in the middle of the room to split it for the boys. One side she decked out with toys and superhero decor for Jesse. The other side she split into *teenage* boy stuff, mainly the Seattle Seahawks, as that was Liam's favorite sports team.

At least once a week, Antoinette would come home after a sixteen-hour-work-and-school day to a homecooked meal with candles lit and her favorite wine poured. She was so stupidly in love with Tanner and it was clouding her judgment. What she didn't realize or differentiate at

the time was that both red flags and butterflies can feel the same. Tanner was working odd jobs, she was never too sure what he was doing for work but his depression was eating him alive. He was on suicide watch and she unfortunately didn't understand what he was going through at all. She mistook his depression for laziness. He hardly slept and it did worry her. He had night terrors when he did sleep and mental demons when he was awake, he couldn't catch a break and Antoinette was at a total loss on what to do. She took it personally thinking that she wasn't enough or that she could fix his mental problems.

Friday nights became their date nights before picking up Jesse for the weekend on Saturday morning. One night, Tanner had convinced Antoinette to try a marijuana gummy. She was always more into alcohol than weed but he could get her to do anything. They bought them from one of her friends' husbands, who mixed the marijuana gummy with Bacardi 151. She was too ignorant to know the difference and Tanner hadn't had an edible in a long time so he decided to use her as a guinea pig. He handed her an entire edible, which looked like a large blue Lego, and told her to eat the whole thing. Little did she know that she was being set up and within an hour she wanted Tanner to take her to the emergency room. She had hit zero gravity and couldn't move because she was so high.

After that night, and realizing what he did to her, she started to only take a third of the gummy on their date nights. They would get high and play Mario Kart on Nintendo 64 until she was so high that Rainbow Road made her dizzy.

"Did you know you have five stages when you're high?" Tanner said to her randomly one Saturday morning after yet another "Pot Gummy Friday."

"What?" Antoinette asked, puzzled.

"Stage one, you're trying not to laugh and get embarrassed from being so high," and she starts blushing instantly.... He loves when she blushes and so he continues, "It's adorable the way you blush and your cheeks smile so hard that they almost cover your eyes. Stage two is the munchies stage. You eat food in literal milliseconds...," *nice job, fatass....* "It's great, you're perfect. Stage three is the nonverbal stage. You won't speak but try to communicate with me through your hands. You refuse to open your mouth and speak. I have no idea why you do it but it is incredibly infuriating...."

At this point she is almost crying. How freaking adorable is he to notice all these things about her.

"...Stage four, you won't move nor allow me to touch you. This is usually when you are coming down from your high and we have to stop playing Mario Kart because you say gravity hits you and you're going to die. It's stupid cute...."

"What's my last stage?" she asks with complete and utter adoration and swoon.

"Your last stage is when gravity takes over and you want to sleep on the couch. I have to move you to the bed and I watch you sleep. It partially sucks because I'm horny and want to eat you up but you are never horny high so I just let you sleep and thank God for putting you in my life."

Mush. Absolute mush. Antoinette's heart exploded and she kissed him. Hard. They had basically broken in every part of the apartment since moving in and she still hadn't gotten sick of his lips. She climbed on top and he was already hard. She slowly moved her thick and full lips to his neck, he was Jell-O in her hands. Before you knew it, he pulled his dick out and she traveled south, kissing every inch of him. He watched her as she moved lower and lower down his body with such desire and gratitude.

Antoinette had never been loved so well before and she wanted to thank him. She started licking the tip first while she massaged him and then, with one motion, put the entire thing in her mouth and deep down her throat. He groaned in pleasure.

"Lick my balls," he requested in between moans.

She was so confused, Antoinette had never done that before. *His balls are by his butthole…get a hold of yourself, you can do this!*

She continued massaging his shaft while she lifted his cock up and licked his balls. He lost his damn mind! She had never seen him get so worked up and squirm so much. It turns her on even more. She loves to spoil him sexually as he does for her. Antoinette continues to lick, suckle and kiss those balls until there's no tomorrow. *He's gonna orgasm like this, I can feel it.* Just as Tanner's about to finish, she sticks her mouth over his tip and lets him explode, swallowing every ounce.

"You are amazing," he says, sweating and panting. Tanner continued to look at her like she's a fucking goddess. *I could really get used to those looks.*

I'm going to quit my job and start a t-shirt printing business. I have all these ideas and with my connections and people skills, I would have so much business.

Antoinette thought she was having a weird dream until she rolled over and Tanner was pacing out of bed, waving his hands in the air, almost frantic. He was already on job #3, or was it 4, since they started dating? Thank God she had a steady good-paying job at the State Representatives to keep them afloat.

Prior to Rushing, he was a paramedic for fifteen years and before that in the Air Force serving our country for four years. Both jobs, surrounded by death, had royally fucked him up mentally and made working a "normal" 9-5 job incredibly difficult to him. Antoinette didn't understand depression at all. She had never battled something so dark and they fought constantly about her lack of empathy and his, what she thought was, laziness. She honestly didn't care if he worked at a damn McDonald's but she just wanted him to work. She could afford him working something small and with minimum wage, just something to get his ass off the bed and get out of the house.

"Baby, why did you quit your job? How are you going to make your own t-shirts without money for start-up costs?"

When he was like this, Antoinette had to tread very carefully. He could go from frantic to angry very fast. He always thought she was trying to bring him down or control his income when in reality she was just trying to be the sane mind in all his chaos.

"I'll get a loan for being a veteran...," he began to lay out his plan.

He honestly was like a crackhead fiending for some drugs when he got like this. She had never seen him so strung out and hyper. He wasn't even making sense and his business ideas were completely bogus. Her stepdad had owned a business since the year she was born and her biological dad was always a bigwig manager for a Fortune 500 company; she knew business. She knew what consumers would want and how to handle business and prepare for it; he was not preparing correctly. But Antoinette would let him rant on and on for well over an hour and said nothing.

Finally, Tanner was done ranting and said, "Well, what do you think?"

She was hesitant to answer that question.

"I like the idea, babe...but, I think that you should get another job right now and save for startup costs. Then work both jobs until the t-shirt thing takes off."

Antoinette could see the disappointment in his eyes and then the anger flooded out. Tanner began pacing some more while she continued to sit, keeping quiet, scared of his anger. He would never physically hurt her like *he* did but he would yell and the vein would pop in his forehead.

"You never support me. You just want me under your thumb so you can control me...," ranting on and on.

Antoinette tried defending herself but he wouldn't listen. He was seeing red. She finally was fed up and lost control of her words just as he did. They were both seeing red, yelling at each other while their pets were hiding in the corner.

"You're fucking crazy!" Antoinette screamed at him.

That word was some sort of trigger because he took the remote and threw it at the wall, leaving a hole in the sliding closet door. She had never seen him *that* angry. With that throw, he walked out the door and Antoinette was on the floor triggered by her own monsters...hiding in the corner on the floor and crying.

Chapter 10

Antoinette walked in his parents' house and went straight to the basement, where his room was. As she entered the hallway, she could smell the vodka. He was Skyping his sister, who was in Mexico with his parents next to him.

"Hola, Angelique! Como estas?" his sister asked when she saw Antoinette walk in.

She hugged and kissed his parents and him while responding to her. Antoinette loved being able to speak Spanish with his family; she truly loved his family.

"Hey, baby, you lookin' hot," he said to her, grabbing her ass.

"Why are you drunk with your parents right here? It's not even four o'clock."

Thankfully, his parents didn't speak English so they both could pretend they weren't fighting with tones and

smiles but say what they wanted and his parents wouldn't know.

He grabbed her arm just above the elbow and squeezed while whispering, "Shut the fuck up. My parents don't know so keep your stupid mouth shut."

Tears began to well up in her eyes. She hated when he got angry with her. He was only squeezing her arm now but once his parents left, he would get angrier if Antoinette didn't suck up and apologize.

She went to the bathroom to have a mini-breakdown so his parents didn't see her crying. She found his liquor bottle under the sink still half full so she emptied it and filled it with water. She always did this when she found his liquor; he never noticed because he was too drunk. She entered the room after her mini-breakdown and they had hung up with his sister. His mom got out of the chair and they were about to leave when his mom looked Antoinette directly in the eyes and she knew. She wiped a tear from her cheek and hugged her tightly. Antoinette wasn't fluent in Spanish yet so they couldn't have full conversations but they spoke with their eyes. His mom knew he was a monster. She was tiny, maybe a hundred pounds soaking wet, and needed insulin shots before every meal due to diabetes. She didn't stand a chance next to him and so she exited the room with his dad.

"What did you say to my mother?" he asked angrily.

"Nothing, baby! You know I can't speak enough Spanish to have a conversation with her."

His hands are squeezing her arms so tight and he has herself pinned against a wall, tears flowing down her face....

Just then, his dad walks in. Short little plump Mexican man with absolutely no fear. He sees his son manhandling a young girl and completely loses his shit. He calls his son out by his full name and pulls him outside the bedroom by his ears and then slams the door. Antoinette

picks up her things, ready to bolt when she can get the chance. She knows she'll be back but for tonight, it's done. She can hear his father screaming at him in Spanish but they're speaking so fast, she can't translate.

What seems like an eternity later, his mom knocks and comes in with such love in her eyes. How did such beautiful people create such a monster? He walks in with his dad still *holding on to his ear. He was bent down sideways because his dad was shorter than him.*

"I'm so sorry for grabbing you like that. It was not the way I was raised, mi amor. Please forgive me."

He has tears in his eyes. He looks genuine. His parents are watching their every move waiting for her to forgive him.

"It's okay," she tells him when it is, in fact, not okay.

They hug her again and apologize for their grown son...but then they left Antoinette alone with him and he fell asleep apologizing to her.

––––––––

Tanner got a job working as a body removal specialist and threw out his t-shirt business

idea...like he had with all the other irrational ones. Antoinette was trying so hard to hold it together but taking care of a grown man with some serious demons and PTSD was a lot more than she really could handle but she wasn't willing to give up on him.

What is a body removal specialist, you ask? Well, when a dead body is found, whether in a crime scene or nursing home, Tanner's job is to go and get the body and deliver it to the funeral home. Tanner was the perfect person for this job. He was the kindest, most respectful and empathetic person Antoinette had ever met. He felt people's pains on a whole 'nother level.

Tanner would be on call for five or six days straight where the calls would come at any hours of the day or night. If there were runs at night, Antoinette would go with him just to spend time with him. She didn't need sleep.

It's 3 A.M. and Tanner gets a call for a body removal. Antoinette is snoring so peacefully with her mouthguard, which helps prevent her from grinding her teeth. Tanner loves watching her sleep and hates to wake her but he knows she would be livid if he did not wake her up for the call. He gently kisses her cheek and tells her there's a call.

Through her mouthguard drool, she slurs "Yes." He gets her clothes and waits for her to get dressed. Antoinette always had an all-black outfit for when she went on these jobs with him. No one ever asked who she was because they were too busy grieving over the loved one they lost.

Forty-five minutes later and they pull into a small dark nursing home: Howell. It's quiet, all the residents are sleeping. Tanner opens up the back of his van and rolls out the bed for the body. Antoinette is finally awake and ready to roll. She really loved this job, actually, and considered being a mortician. She was always fascinated (not in a creepy way) and intrigued about who the person was before they died. Tanner was always surprised by her, constantly keeping him on his toes. He was also surprised by how interested Antoinette was in death. Little did he know she also had demons she was hiding.

They walk in the room where the body is, making sure to be very quiet and not wake the other residents. The nice nurse has tears in her eyes as she points to the body. Ninety-seven-year-old man with no family. No visitors, no friends, no one to miss him. Those were the ones that hurt Tanner and Antoinette the most: having no one to love you during your last days.

Tanner undressed him, leaving just the underwear. They carefully grab his body and pull him by the edge of his sheets onto the rolling bed. Tanner gently covers the body with blankets followed by a silent prayer. Antoinette always loved watching him work like this. Such care and tenderness. They zip up the body bag, load him into the van and head to the funeral home. The funeral home was back near their house and Antoinette had never been to this one before.

This funeral home was like the nursing home: small and beautiful. Tanner always had a keycode or something to get into these places when no one was there. They wheeled the body into the back door and then Antoinette saw a pallet with chains hanging over the basement floor. Clearly puzzled, Tanner showed her what they had to do to lower the body and take it downstairs to the fridge.

Why didn't this funeral home just build an elevator like most? This is so old school.

While in the big body freezer Tanner had to do paperwork, so Antoinette looked around like the weirdo that she was. There were four bodies on the main tables either embalmed already or preparing to be embalmed. Each had a photo next to their head with what their loved ones wanted them to look like. One of the bodies was a lovely old lady whose makeup made her look like a clown. *This isn't at all like the photo! Her family is going to be so disappointed!* Her determined ass started to look around and tried to find whatever makeup they used. She wished she had bought her own makeup.

"What are you doing?" Tanner scared the shit out of her as she was looking through their makeup closet.

"Trying to find the makeup they use so I can fix the lady in the freezer."

"You're not doing that, come on. You don't work here, you could get arrested for tampering with a body or something!"

"I promise you the family won't press charges against herself once I'm done. She looks terrible!" Antoinette was practically begging at this point but she knew he was right.

"Baby, come on. You're sweet but we can't do this. Let's go."

She huffed and puffed.

"Tanner...you know... I've never had sex in a funeral home." she said to him with a large smile and lust in her eyes.

His jaw dropped.

"Absolutely not! That is so disrespectful! I am not going to Hell for that."

Antoinette was not getting anything she wanted tonight and this princess was not happy about it.

Chapter 11

It was almost Christmas, their second one together and their one-year anniversary. They were spending the month of December prior to Christmas at various "Friendsgiving" events, mostly of her friends. But Phil and Rex from Black Rebels MC invited Tanner and Antoinette to one of their "family" dinners. Family as in the MC family. Absolutely zero part of Antoinette wanted to attend this event. She didn't like Rex, didn't care for Phil and didn't want Tanner in this club. Between his mental illness getting worse and her lack of trust in him escalating, she just felt like it was a bad idea and that thought process was written all over her face.

Antoinette tried to put her feelings aside and just enjoy the evening. There were kids everywhere, which was her favorite part She bonded with Phil's three-year-old granddaughter that was *almost* as cute as Jesse. She was attached to Antoinette's hip the entire night. Dinner was cooked okay with your basic Thanksgiving foods: turkey, mashed potatoes, stuffing, cranberry sauce, etc. Tanner was in the high of his life, being treated like royalty. He was meeting potential club members and their families; he was overjoyed and excited. Antoinette was in a fairly decent mood but still had her walls up. She liked most of the people she met and there wasn't any pressure about Tanner joining...yet.

Dessert came around, a plethora of pies, and Phil started tapping his beer bottle for an announcement.

"TK, we are so glad you are here with your old lady. We have thoroughly enjoyed getting to know you and your heart. You are the perfect fit for this family."

Next thing you know, Rex comes out with a leather vest with "Prospect" patched on the back just like in *Sons of Anarchy*. Tanner started to cry tears of joy when they handed it to him. Everyone then looked at Antoinette. She smiled but they knew she was faking it. She has always worn her emotions on her face and there was no denying her feelings, she had the worst poker face. Antoinette really wanted to be happy for Tanner and she knew it broke his heart for him to see her face like that, but she didn't know how. He would later say it was all about control but Antoinette didn't see it that way. When you love someone, you want to protect them. You want to make sure they aren't deceived, taken advantage of or hurt in any way. While car accidents happen daily, Antoinette was a worry wart about motorcycles and believed he would die on one. *He doesn't even have a bike, how is he supposed to be a damn prospect?* Her look of disgust that night would later haunt their relationship until the very end and Tanner wouldn't forget her for it.

After that disastrous night, Antoinette wanted to make up for it by planning a big one-year anniversary gift for them. How had it already been a year? Liam was moving back from New Mexico after the first of the year and she was about to become a full-time stepmom of an eleven-year-old. It was also right around the end of her first semester of law school and

her law school was putting on a winter ball for their students. It was free for the students and just $50 per guest. It also included food, alcohol and dancing, plus it was a formal tie event and Antoinette loved any excuse to dress up.

This winter ball was at Detroit's Motor City Casino and Hotel, which was absolutely gorgeous. Antoinette decided to book a night there after the winter ball for their anniversary trip with a nice long couples' massage the next day in Motor City Casino's spa. Tanner knew about the hotel room but not about the spa and she was giddy with anticipation to spoil him.

They checked in the night of the ball a little early so that she could get ready. She had a floor-length black lace dress with a beige liner that made her look naked underneath. It was tighter around her stomach than she had hoped but she tried to ignore it because it made her breasts look amazing. She had dyed her Jessica Rabbit red hair back to brunette and curled it with a smokey eye and red lipstick. Tanner wanted to rip the dress right off of her once he saw her in it and she gave in as usual. This time she stayed on top so that she wouldn't ruin her hair.

Before they headed to the ball downstairs, they took three shots of Fireball Whiskey each in the hotel room. They were tipsy, horny and happy. It was going to be a phenomenal weekend. Antoinette introduced Tanner to all of the classmates she liked and they kept drinking. However, for every drink Antoinette had, Tanner had two. The ball ended at 10 P.M. and she was ready to devour her man in the hotel room but Tanner had other plans in mind. Tipsy Tanner wanted to gamble. He wanted to drink and gamble. He didn't want to spend time with her but she tried to stay calm. An hour later, and she was most definitely done being calm.

"Baby, can we go upstairs and hang out? I'm horny and it's our anniversary," she said to him with his baby begging eyes.

"No. I want to keep trying to get money for us." He wasn't winning and was wasting his money and the money she spent on the hotel room.

"I don't want the money. I just want time with you."

He ignored her so she got mad and started to walk away.

Five minutes later, she sees out of the corner of her eye his drunk ass wobbling besides her.

"You are such a fun sucker. Why do you have to ruin everything?" he says to her.

"Ruin everything? I paid for this hotel room, our dinner and everything else to make this weekend special for us. One would think that you could put the drink down and focus on your girl, who just spent a fortune on you."

"Yes, yes. You are so perfect. You spoil me and buy everything for me. You are the best ever and my loser ass doesn't deserve you."

At this point, he's being loud enough for other people in the casino to hear and she kept walking toward the hotel room. If he wants to argue, he can follow her upstairs and they can argue. She isn't some white-trash princess who wants an audience for their fights. And he does follow her. And they do fight and come to no happy conclusion. Happy fucking anniversary.

Antoinette slams the door of the bathroom and starts the shower. She is crying with anger at this point but also secretly hoping he comes in and fixes things so their anniversary doesn't get completely ruined. He is the worst when he drinks liquor. His anger fuels her anger and it's like those Eminem lyrics—*when a volcano meets a tornado*, that is them. Antoinette is the tornado; cold, devastating and powerful when she crosses your path. He is the volcano, a hothead who is beautiful and calm from afar but can be set off so easily and causes so much

damage. Together, they both can create this immensely large and destructive storm. Storms are beautiful to look at but you don't want to be smack dab in the middle of a volcano and tornado. It's deadly.

Forty-five minutes in the hot shower and he never came in... she walked out and he was asleep, snoring like a log. Deja vu, she's been through this shit before and she just continues to ignore those red flags.

———

It's the night before Valentine's and they booked a hotel room. Antoinette had never gotten a hotel room with a guy before. While they had been dating for almost a year, it was still new and super "adulty" for her being freshly eighteen. They went to get dinner at Red Robin, saw a movie and headed back to the hotel room for some drinks. He had always gotten the cheapest vodka, which tasted like rubbing alcohol. She didn't realize how cheap he was until she turned 21 and saw it for herself.

Valentine's morning and they both had to work around 11 A.M. She woke up hungover as shit around 7:00 A.M. and went looking for pills. Any bottle of pills to help with this hangover before she had to work a ten-hour shift. His phone kept buzzing.... Who has been messaging him all night? She picks up his Blackberry as he's sleeping soundly on the bed. She just wanted to check to make sure it wasn't a family emergency...or so she told herself.

Antoinette unlocked his phone and went to his messages. All she saw was female names. One after another of female names. Why was he talking to so many females? Wait a minute...Tammy? As in Ex-girlfriend Tammy? Don't click the message. Do not click them.

Damn it, she clicked it.

"How is Charlie?"

Why is he asking about her kid....

"He is doing great! He is already rolling over. He would love to meet you!"

This kid is like six months old, all he cares about is the tits that feed him. He has no desire to meet his mommy's ex-boyfriend....

"I would love to meet him too. When are you free this week?"

Antoinette stopped reading. She was seeing red. Why in the actual fuck would you 1) be texting your ex-girlfriend, 2) asking to see her baby that they at one point were concerned was his, and 3) texting to your ex-girlfriend. Yes, that important factor needs repeating. This asshat drunk doesn't even let Antoinette see her best guy friend from high school because apparently guys and girls can't be friends but he can make plans to see his ex-girlfriend? The red was just getting redder, if that is possible.

Antoinette can't confront him. He's never hurt her sober but what if he is still drunk? They're alone in a hotel room, it isn't safe. She can't confront him and risk his anger overshadowing her anger....

So she quietly gets dressed, grabs her shit and walks out. She texts her best friend for a ride and then blows his shit up via text. At least he can't hurt her at work....

————

"I think we should get Liam," Antoinette told Tanner.

She had been telling him for months now that they were getting him come January and he didn't believe her but this time she meant business. It was time. Liam had now been back in New Mexico for about a year and had spent the last few months begging Tanner to come back. He said he was miserable. He

continued to claim that his mom made him drink beer and smoke cigarettes. Whether that was true or he was lying, that kid needed a stable environment.

"You're not ready, we're not ready," Tanner tried to explain to Antoinette as he was pacing in their bedroom.

Regardless if we were ready or not, I cannot leave this kid there any longer but I am not making that drive again... SIX HUNDRED DOLLARS?? To fly a kid one way from New Mexico? Antoinette made decent money but she definitely didn't have that kind of money to just throw around. *Think, think, think.... IDEA!*

Antoinette started a GoFundMe page to get Liam up. So many people donated, including her parents, which shocked her the most. Her mom donated $250 toward his plane ticket. Liam's mom said she'd send him up for $4,000. Yes, she was offering to sell her kid to Tanner and Antoinette. They ended up only raising $2,700 and she took it and sent her son on a plane to live with them for that $2,700. "Mother of the Year" award.

Antoinette spent the weeks after their fucked-up anniversary trip preparing everything for Liam. She ordered him an all-black desk with a lime green chair (his favorite color) for homework. She bought him new clothes, games, hygiene products, books and more. She maxed out one of her credit cards preparing for his arrival.

The first few nights after Liam arrived were...complicated, to say the least. He was *terrified.* The reservation he came from told a ridiculous amount of scary bonfire stories to their kids. He believed all sorts of spirits were haunting him and his dreams and he was terrified to be alone. Coming from a separated family, Antoinette was pretty sure he used that as an excuse to steal his dad's attention but she let him. Liam slept on the floor by their bed the first week he was with them. No sex for them.

Shortly thereafter, Tanner made him start sleeping in his own room but they had given him multiple nightlights and left their doors open in case he needed to come in. Their sex life was nonexistent. *Is this what kids do?* By week two, Antoinette was already exhausted from being a full-time stepmom but she was also thankful. Thankful that Liam was safe and with them. Little did she know this kid was the beginning of the end for their relationship.

————

One short month later, Antoinette soon realized what a compulsive liar Liam was. Who knows if anything he told them about his mom was true and Tanner was too damn soft on him. Every time Antoinette gave her opinion, Tanner would say that Liam needed time to adjust and he had a hard life. *Yes, he had a hard life but he also needed rules and boundaries. He was twelve, he could do some chores. Shit, we even had Jesse, who was six, do some chores when he came over.*

Antoinette paid $150 for a weeklong basketball camp. Liam said he loved basketball and Antoinette wanted him to get outside and make some friends, be active. After the first day, Liam cried so hard to Tanner that he didn't make him go again. He had asked for this basketball camp. *When I asked for things as a kid, my parents would give it to me but if I didn't want to finish, too bad.* There was no reason he couldn't finish the next four days and not waste her money. He loved basketball, he just wanted to sit at home and sleep. But Tanner insisted. And who was she? Not his mom, clearly.

"This kid has been through enough. He needs more time to adjust."

If I had a dollar for every time I heard this bullshit.

"How is he going to adjust to anything if you just let him stay bottled up inside this apartment every day?" Antoinette could see his face turning red.

"You are not his damn mother. I am his father and I will make the decisions."

You're the father? You don't know if he is even biologically yours. I got him here, I paid

for everything he has, I signed him up for school, I paid for the camp, I buy all the gro-
ceries, I took him for his eye exam and doctor's checkup. I'm more of a fucking parent
than you are.

Don't worry, Antoinette didn't say all that out loud but damn, her blood
was boiling. Problem with dating someone with severe mental illness?
You can't always say what you want to say. They can't always handle the
truth. Antoinette could see Liam pretending to have his headphones in
but he was listening. She felt pretty sure that he was snickering too—
her loss and his gain. He had his dad wrapped around his fingers and not
in a good way.

———

To help alleviate the tension that was clearly brewing in their home,
Tanner planned a camping trip for the whole family. As you could have
guessed, Antoinette was not a fan of camping but agreed to attend for
the sake of their relationship. *Camping is disgusting. There are bugs and gross*
bathrooms and no bed. The sweat. The outhouses. Fuck this. For men, it is easier.
They can just whip their dick out and pee wherever they'd like. What
do you do when you camp? You drink. And what happens when you have
to break the seal? You have to pee constantly. Who wants to be peeing
constantly in an outhouse? Antoinette was a city girl through and
through. She was dreading this trip.

Antoinette, Tanner, the boys and her dog Beau were supposed to drive
in one car up north. However, with Tanner's camping obsession, it took
two cars due to all of his gear and camping materials. Already grumpy,
Antoinette was forced to drive four hours up north in a car alone with
some camping supplies and Beau. Beau was a Maltese-poodle mix. He
had the Maltese face but the poodle nose and she had had him since she
was sixteen. He went everywhere with her—summers in Florida with
her dad, Tennessee when she lived there for a year, when she lived with

him, when she lived on her own before Tanner and then when she lived with Tanner. Beau was her day one and would pick him over anyone on the planet. Remember how wrecked she was when Sugar died? When that day ever comes for Beau, it will be the end of her soul as she knows it. She won't ever be the same after that loss.

The drive to anywhere up north in Michigan, whether it be the top of the lower peninsula or the upper peninsula, is beautiful. Unpopulated areas of Michigan are gorgeous. Lakes everywhere, trees, wildlife. One day, she would love to live up there. Antoinette also invited AJ and her boyfriend, Jim, to come and meet them up there. Antoinette was also hoping that AJ would keep her attitude in check.

Once they arrived in the two cars, it was pouring outside. Not just some rain, but a total tsunami outside. Tanner's former paramedic friends who were also joining them were already there and waiting. No surprise, they were all female. Tanner starts to unpack his car and tries to set up the tent in the rain. His paramedic female friends are flocking to his rescue to help him while Antoinette's city girl petty ass sits in the car. *Ain't no way I am getting soaked in the dirt after I drove four hours up here alone. I need a damn drink.*

It finally stopped raining and the first night was a joke, as expected. AJ, her dog, and Jim didn't arrive until 11 P.M. and Tanner was already belligerent drunk, telling all his old EMS and Navy stories with the girls. Neither of them minded, they were eyeing him like the hot piece of

blue-eyed candy he was and Antoinette was obviously not a fan of women fawning over her man. *Why do people camp? Like really. Why would anyone want to sleep on an air mattress, in a stuffy tent when you can get a hotel room with bathrooms right there? It makes no sense to me.*

The following day, AJ and Tanner's female friends spent half the day arguing about dogs. It was ridiculous. Tanner's friends were being very aggressive about dog breeds and how to train them and AJ was standing up for her very well-behaved and beautiful dog, Lily. *As she should. Talk shit about my dog and see what happens.* Tanner was wasted again the entire day and would constantly whisper to her that he was "done," only to sober up later and apologize. He was really starting to remind her of *him... but at least he didn't physically hurt me. He would never physically hurt me....*

It was finally the last night of their God-forsaken camping trip and Antoinette was *really* trying to have a good time but also counting down the hours until they were back home. She had one too many drinks and headed to the bathroom. If it wasn't for Jesse and Liam, she would've peed in a bush. It was a three-minute walk minimum through a pitch-black and creepy-ass campground. The bathrooms were not the worst she had seen camping but they were still not her cup of tea. She finished peeing and when she opened the stall, Tanner was there. He was swaying back and forth drunk and his eyes were full of lust. He turned her around and bent her ass over the toilet. *This is not fucking sanitary.* He didn't bother wetting her up like usual before he rammed his cock inside of her.

"Who's Daddy's girl?" he asked her while ramming inside of her.

"I am, baby," she responded but wished she wasn't.

"You're a dirty fucking whore. MY dirty fucking whore," he said while pulling her hair and finishing inside of her.

No orgasm for her and apparently she was a whore. How much longer until they are home again?

"Babe...I really didn't like you calling me a whore," Antoinette tried to say empathetically on their walk back to the campsite.

"But you are a whore. You're my whore," he said with no desire to understand her feelings.

Tanner had never spoken to her like that. He was always so kind and gentle in nature. These people and all the alcohol turned him into someone completely different. Someone Antoinette had already been with before... someone she didn't want to ever be with again.

———

He stumbles down the stairs. He's drunk again. She pretends to be asleep in hopes that he doesn't wake and get angry. He gets naked and lays in bed. He starts to caress her thighs and ass. He reeks of whiskey.

"Wake up," he whispers.

That's an order. She pretended that she was sleeping and yawned.

"I'm tired, babe. I work in the morning," she said to try and get out of it.

He rolls her over and gets on top.

"I'm not tired," he says as he starts to rub his hard cock against her thigh.

"Don't you love me?" he continues.

"Of course I do."

"Then let me in."

And she does. Anything to keep him calm. Anything to prevent bruises.

"Good girl. That's my little sexy Cuban whore."

He pulls her hair and thrusts harder. Soon he'll be done and pass out. Sexy Cuban whore.

Chapter 12

Tanner quit his body removal specialist job that Antoinette loved. She loved him in a sexy black suit. She loved going on calls with him. She loved the pay. But at this point, his mental illness and PTSD were running his life and he did not bother fighting it anymore. He accepted his *fucked-upness* and was letting it eat him alive. Again, Antoinette didn't understand it. She didn't understand how someone could lay around all day every day not doing anything. They had bills to pay.

"I have a proposition for you...," he says to her the morning after he quit his job.

Fishy....

"You work and pay the bills, I'll stay home and cook and clean. With my depression, I can't work right now but you can make me lists and I can do side jobs."

Um, hell yes. No cooking or cleaning for her? Yes, please. Fuck gender roles; sugar momma life, here I come.

The idea was nice but the execution didn't follow through. Day one and she came home to nothing done. Same with day two. *Okay, he's enjoying his little vacation. Let's give him a few days to chill.* His weed intake has also increased 200% if not more since he had succumbed to his mental demons. He smokes anywhere from 5-8 bowls a day to "help with his depression" but he is totally self-diagnosed with no desire to seek real medical advice.

Day four: "Baby, how is my list coming?"

"I just woke up an hour ago." It was 2 P.M.

"I'm going to get Liam from school, get my medicine (his pot) and then come home and cook us dinner."

"Okay, maybe tomorrow you could start the list?"

"I'll do your stupid fucking list when I have time," he says.

"When do you have time? You have all day. You literally do nothing!" Antoinette had had it.

"I am trying to survive!" he screams.

"Survive from what? A roof over your head, clothes on your back, food on your belly? A woman who loves you completely and is supporting both you and your kids so you can get better?"

"You just don't fucking get it. Get the pain I feel every day."

"Go see a damn doctor then!"

"Fuck the doctors!" he says and then bam. His fist into the wall. Clear whole in the wall and his knuckles are red.

He walks out and Antoinette is on the floor shaking. *These panic attacks are becoming too much lately.* They remind her so much of when she was on the floor shaking because of *him.* She sat there for a while, not sure how long. Beau came and sat next to her, giving her kisses. She zoned out remembering all the times *he* had left her on the floor crying. How did she end up in this same spot twice already? *What is wrong with me?*

With Tanner's depression, the boys had not done shit all summer except for one or two camping trips. She always asked what he wanted to do this weekend since they only had Jesse two days a week but he never wanted to go anywhere or do anything. He was high all day and never left the house. Sex life was also caput. He needed professional help and Antoinette was so confused on what to do or how to help. He had broken up with her at least half a dozen times, twice in front of the kids. This was no way for any of them to live.

One morning Antoinette got so fed up that she called his ass out and said bullshit to all this depression drama. Note here: Never say that to someone suffering. Really suffering. After Antoinette told him he was full of shit when he said he wanted to kill himself, Tanner decided to attempt to commit suicide in front of her by swallowing a bottle of pills. Attention seeking? Maybe. Terrifying? Absolutely. She threatened to call 9-1-1, so he forced himself to throw up and drank milk. Who knew that drinking milk helps digest an entire bottle of pills? Ever since then, Antoinette kept her mouth shut about his depression and seeking professional medical help.

Tanner isn't like him. He doesn't get drunk and hit me. He gets mad and hits the wall. It's okay. It's different.

––––––––––

After that pill bottle incident, Tanner finally voluntarily admitted himself for a week at the Veterans Affairs Psychiatric Hospital. She had now become a full-time single mom to a kid only twelve years younger than her. The first three days of the psych hold and he couldn't talk to anyone outside of the hospital. He had to focus on getting "sober" from all the pot and try out different pharmaceuticals. Antoinette and Liam had a system down now. Once she arrived home from work, he would work on the summer bridge book she bought him to prepare for school while she cooked dinner. Then they would eat, watch TV, and then she would have him turn off all electronics one hour before bed in which case he would read. A book. Yes, kids read! They would often read together on the couch before he went to bed. She read somewhere that no

screen time for an hour before bed helps relax the brain and prepare to sleep better. It was probably the first time Liam had had a routine his entire life and she was enjoying the bonding time. They never argued, he did as he was told and they were getting along really well. It had only been three days but still. She felt like a damn good stepmom.

On the third day, right when she was allowed to, she called the VA and asked to speak to him. He sounded good. He sounded peaceful. Antoinette was instantly relieved and hopeful. She asked when she could see him and he encouraged her to come now. She told her boss she had a family emergency and headed straight to the VA.

She couldn't wait to see him. She really wanted to jump his bones but they don't allow any visitors in the bedrooms. When she walked in, she had to check her purse at the counter with the front desk. She couldn't bring anything in, including her phone. It was all worth it when she looked up and she saw him walking down the hallway toward her. Both of them grinning up to their eyes, Antoinette hardly able to breathe. All the stress of being a single mom faded away as she almost fell to the ground at the sight of him.

When they hugged, the world melted away and she felt home. She was crying with joy and everyone was watching. He wiped away her tears, grabbed her hand and began giving her a tour of the place. Tanner showed her the cafeteria, library, common space and game room. He introduced her to the other guys he made friends with, and it was nothing like you would expect a *loony bin* to feel or look like. These were all just brave men who fought for our country and had been mentally destroyed by it. There was a sense of peace and hope in there.

After the tour, Tanner asked Antoinette to meet with the psychologist he had been working with. She felt uncomfortable with the entire meeting. She was not his wife (even if she acted like it) and they had been so rocky lately. She felt as though she was invading his very personal space. The psychologist treated Tanner with such respect and compassion. The meeting, while uncomfortable, made Antoinette feel like his wife for real and she was surprisingly okay with it. She also felt a sense of "everything is going to be okay."

After the meeting, the two just sat down on chairs in the hallway and stared in each other eyes like those stupid mushy movies. They only had thirty minutes left until they were going to kick Antoinette out for visiting hours and she was already starting to feel the separation anxiety.

"You're giving me the look. Stop giving me the look. We can't have sex now, you know that," he says to her through his adorable dimples, making her blush. Shit, even he's blushing knowing what she wants to do in front of all these people.

Antoinette nonchalantly puts her Michael Kors leather jacket over Tanner's lap and starts to slowly move her hand to his leg. His eyes widened and his cheeks blushed more. She then slips her hands under his hospital scrub like pants and reaches his hot, sweaty dick.

"Baby, what are you doing?!" he whispers to her, face beet red.

"Shhh...act natural," she whispers back with a wicked grin on her face.

Antoinette begins to caress his dick as it gets hard. Normally you would need some kind of lubricant like spit or lotion but she was hellbent on making it happen. Rubbing and rubbing
him, staring directly into his eyes, he gets solid hard. His breathing is heavier...labored as he tries to act natural, she is wet watching him in all his glory. She slips her fingers past his shaft and heads for his balls and his sweet spot past them. Watching him squirm was her favorite thing to do, he was fucking beautiful.

She goes back to caressing him and is so horny watching his facial expressions knowing he is getting pleasure under her leather jacket. People are walking by, smiling and saying hello, without a clue in the world. His breathing gets heavier and now his chest is noticeably rising and falling. He is almost here. Antoinette goes in to pretend to whisper in his ear but surprises him instead with a lick around his ear. Tanner lets out a moan and squeezes her other hand.

"Are you going to cum for me, baby?" she whispers to him as an orderly walks by completely ignorant.

At that moment, as he is getting ready to finish, no one else is in that room. It is just them and their eyes are locked as he explodes into her hand...and his pants. He uses his hands to cover his face and lets out a big sigh of relief as his face turns lobster red realizing there is semen all over his thighs and in his pants. He is speechless that that just happened. She jacked him off in a psych ward and she got high off that adrenaline.

"I love you, I'll call you when I get home," Antoinette says as she gets up and walks out, smiling to herself with pride, leaving him sitting there, dumbfounded.

As she picks up her purse and phone from the front desk, she has a few messages from a number not saved in her phone.

"Beau is just as cute as I remember. Who is that boy with you? Did you adopt a Mexican while I was gone, mi amor?"

Fuck. Fuck. Fuck. How did he find me?

Chapter 13

School started halfway through Tanner's psych stay and Antoinette had gotten Liam into a highly ranked charter school. It was the sister school of a chart school she had gone to as a kid. Tanner's mom took Liam school shopping for uniforms, which surprised the hell out of both of them. She was not particularly a fan of Liam. She had always said he wasn't biologically Tanner's, so she wouldn't treat him as such. Liam did horrible in school down in New Mexico and as an academic nerd herself, Antoinette was determined to change that. He was entering 6th grade with the reading level of a 4th grader and math level of a 3rd grader. She hooked him up with a tutor and studied with him every night.

She really didn't know why she was still with Tanner's certifiably crazy ass other than she loved him. She had learned the hard way long ago with *him* that love wasn't always enough. Your love cannot change a man. Their love for you could potentially change them but your love alone won't change them. Maybe it is the world-altering, freaky-deaky, delicious sex that they had constantly? Is THAT enough to stay with someone? She didn't know that either.

"Babe, I need you to log onto my Facebook and grab a phone number for me," Tanner asked while they were on the phone.

While in the psych ward, he wasn't allowed any internet or cell phones. Antoinette instantly was not a fan of going on his phone, she had never done it before. Every single time you go through a man's phone, you are going to find something. EVERY. SINGLE. TIME. It's a fact. Did you know that when your brain has a trauma of some kind, every time something similar triggers you, your brain automatically goes into fight mode? So when she used to go through *his* phone and find stuff constantly, it created a mental trauma and trigger. Man, her trigger warnings were on high alert when Tanner asked her to go into his phone and she felt nauseous just at the idea. Antoinette had the angel on her right side telling her not to go through his messages and to respect his privacy. But with the angel comes the devil and she had the devil on her left saying, "You a single stepmom, sis, you deserve to know if he's treating you right." She listened to the devil. And she was seeing red.

"Hello, VA Psychiatric Care, how may I direct your call?"

"Yes, can I be transferred to Tanner Kazynek, please?"

"One moment, please...."

"Hey, baby, what's up?"

"You want to tell me why I am sitting here working full time, going to law school, taking care of YOUR son and you're talking dirty to some chick I don't know back in July when I was in Arizona BURYING my dead aunt?"

Red, y'all. Red. No bullshit games, cutting straight to it. Y'all ain't ever seen the Latina crazy come out yet. He gave herself some bullshit answer about how they were fighting the whole trip and it wasn't totally inappropriate. And that he's not even attracted to her. This girl was the beginning of the end for them and he didn't even realize it. That day, she told him she was done and when his ass got out of the psych ward he needed to find a new place to live. She had a man show her no respect for four years and it took her another four years of being single to heal, she was not about to let any man disrespect her now. Like Deepti said in *Love Is Blind*, Season 2, "I know I deserve better…I have no fucking regrets."

———

He came home about three days later. No "Welcome Home" banner or blow job. Antoinette had already started to pack his shit. She was infuriated. He tried to kiss her ass, tried to love her, and she just pushed him away. According to him, he went to a bonfire with her and other people and nothing happened. Meanwhile, Antoinette was 2,000 miles away in Arizona and had no clue till months later that he even went to a bonfire in the first place. Did he cheat? She'll never know.

Liam still had to eat so Antoinette acted civil and started cooking, still making Liam do his homework before any phone time. She kept hearing Facebook Messenger ding nonstop. She listens to the devil on that shoulder again and follows the sounds of his phone, which was on the kitchen table. She didn't go through it but she could see on the lock screen who they are from: It's Bonfire Girl. Tanner is telling *her* how mad Antoinette is and how they keep fighting. How he's struggling to stay alive after leaving the hospital and that Antoinette needs to understand and forgive him.

Why is he telling them to her? And how are they having this conversation without his phone? Your laptop, you idiot. In a blind rage, Antoinette went on a hunt to find him in their tiny apartment.

This almost forty-year-old man is found sitting on the floor in their closet on her laptop. Not his laptop, hers. He swears to her that he was having a panic attack and needed to be dark and quiet. Antoinette throws him his phone and tells him go ahead and just to move in with *Bonfire Girl.*

"Next time you want to have a secret conversation with your side chick, take your phone with you so you don't get caught."

The cat claws were out. Big mistake.

He comes out shortly thereafter, screaming at Liam to go outside and take Beau for a walk. *Great.* Antoinette sits down in the recliner and puts on *General Hospital.* Her guilty pleasure since she was fifteen. She puts the volume up nice and loud so he knows that she doesn't want to talk. He goes into the boys' room, where his clothes are (all of hers took up the main closet), and she starts to see clothes quite literally being thrown out of the bedroom and into the hallway.

"You want to kick me and my boys out? Fine. We'll end up on the streets before we come back here to your psycho, jealous ass."

She ignores him. More clothes go flying.

"You call me crazy? You are fucking crazy. Am I not allowed to have female friends? She's been through this before, she understands what I am going through. Your entitled ass does not! You haven't struggled a day in your life."

If only he knew...but she continues to ignore him.

"Don't worry, princess. We'll be gone tonight. You won't ever have to see us again." Tanner is just shoving trash bags full of clothes in them. His face is beat red.

"All you had to do was say you didn't cheat on me and convince me of it," she said coolly.

"Of course I didn't cheat on your crazy ass. You'd probably cut my dick off if I did."

Accurate but not quite convincing.

"Why are you hanging out with females and not telling me while I'm 2000 miles away? How would you like it if I did that to you?"

She's trying to keep back the tears. He's still shoving garbage bags full of his shit.

"Get over yourself, princess. The world doesn't revolve around you. If I want to have female friends and hang out with them while you're away, I can!"

BAM. He slams his fist on their glass kitchen table. Another big mistake. That glass table is about an inch thick—Antoinette's boujee mom gave it to them. You can tell by his cringe that it's an instant regret on his part. Antoinette chuckles. His knuckles were shattered and she definitely did not get him any ice.

———

Antoinette had her tonsils taken out earlier and was off for three weeks! If you know anything about your tonsils being taken out at nineteen, you know it is so painful. She had gauze in each cheek as her throat was bleeding from the incisions. She couldn't eat anything but mashed-up food and ice cream but even that hurt. All she did was chew gum to help keep her mouth wet but without having to swallow. Not living at home was great until she felt like shit and wanted her mommy to take care of her.

"You would think my boyfriend would be the one to do so but you know what he did that night after he got off work? He went bowling," she thought to herself.

Antoinette had begged him to come by and take care of her and he said he would after he went bowling. She lost her shit. She packed up his stuff and left it on the porch and told him to not come by. After lots of liquid narcotics and crying, she finally fell asleep through the pain.

She woke up to a tumble down the stairs. He's here and he's drunk. How did he even get in? Was the door left unlocked? *She literally just broke up with his ass a few hours ago (for the three hundredth time). He's chuckling as he picks himself up from the stair landing and tries to walk a straight line down the rest of the stairs. He makes it without any injuries. It's black in her room, she likes to sleep in complete darkness. But it's also a mess. Shoes, clothes, dog bones. Part of her wanted him to trip and smash his head but the other part of her was in so much pain that she was just glad he was there....*

"Hi, baby. I'm here," as he whispers into her ear apologetically.

"How did you get in?" she asked. Stubborn and still mad as hell. Apparently the door was unlocked. She asked how bowling was. So mad.

"Baby, I'm so sorry. I know I shouldn't have gone but they were expecting me. I shouldn't have gone. I'm so sorry. Let me take care of you." He had brought her flowers and a tub of her favorite mint chocolate chip ice cream.

She told him to fuck off...while he was drunk...she should've known better. Those apologies turned into words of hate real fast. He whipped her around so fast that it sent her jaw vibrating. Oh, the pain. Hands on her upper arms, his usual position, he's sitting on top of her.

"You little bitch. You think that just because you had your tonsils taken out that you can talk to me how you want? I should make you pay for that. Stupid cunt."

Antoinette can smell the vodka as he screams in her face. It's always vodka—and the cheap kind too. She is in so much pain, tears start rolling. His arms are still firmly on hers, knees pressing deep into her thighs. She can feel her throat bleeding.

"Oh, quit that crying bullshit."

She desperately just wants him to leave. She apologizes over and over again. The blood is now on her lips. She really needs her pain meds.

He gets up wobbly, almost falls down. "You wanna break up because I went bowling? Fine, fuck you."

He throws his apology roses in her face and storms out. She hears the door shut and she quickly runs up to lock it. Thank God that's all he did, she thought to herself. A big sigh of relief as she realizes how lucky she just got. She takes more liquid painkillers, gets an ice pack and cries softly until she passes out.

———

Tanner finally gave up on the stay-at-home dad bit and got a job with insulation. You know, that pink bumpy stuff that goes in attics. And yes, he unpacked all the trash bags of clothes that he angrily threw around. And double yes, her dumb ass just took him back and

tried to move on from the incident. This job had him traveling pretty frequently all over the state. Four days here, seven days there. She was in full-time mommy mode again but also not trusting that he was actually working... not after that texting escapade.

Antoinette continued with Liam's schedule and routine. He read books, did his homework, helped with the dishes, had phone time and video game time all in limited intervals. It was a lot but it worked. Well, for the days Tanner was gone it worked. He'd then come home and throw her schedule all to shit. He'd let Liam do whatever he wanted—sleep in till noon, play on his phone all day; it drove Antoinette bonkers! *But I'm his dad, I can do what I want.* Insert ultimate eye roll here.

Tanner left for a nine-day trip for work in Traverse City. Did Antoinette think he was sleeping with other girls or lying? Every day. Is that because she might also be crazy? Yep, absolutely. Tanner isn't the only one with red flags. Five days into this work trip she was taking Liam to University of Michigan Children's Hospital for severe stomach pains. Tanner was five hours away and incredibly difficult to get a hold of. Antoinette tried her hardest to remain calm. She had to, right? For Liam. But inside, she didn't feel adult enough for this.

I am not old enough to be taking a twelve-year-old kid to the hospital and be the sole parent. Poor Liam had to get x-rays and all sorts of tests done. Come to find out he had serious poop blockage all the way up his intestines. So much poop that it was like he hadn't pooped in weeks. When we asked him about it, he would say he didn't have to go. You are trained to pay attention to if your baby is pooping or a dog but not a teenage boy. One would *assume* they are doing their business.

Tanner came as soon as he could and it was a huge relief for Antoinette when he arrived. Liam had to stay for three days in the hospital and University of Michigan's Children's Hospital is beautiful! Each child gets their own room with every play system and unlimited movies.

Antoinette watched Tanner and Liam play video games and stayed the night there with them. It was the first time she had felt really connected to Liam since he moved back. *Maybe Tanner can get better mentally, hold a job, and we can make this work....*

Chapter 14

They were headed to Vegas, baby! They're getting married.... Just kidding!

Antoinette was headed to Las Vegas with her mom to see her all-time favorite female singer: Celine Freaking Dion! They got tickets for second row. Second. Row. Antoinette was so geeked. This was her sixth time seeing Celine in concert and second time going to Vegas just to see her. Celine Dion is a goddess queen.

A lot of her fangirl joy was overshadowed by her destructive and toxic love life. Tanner and her had decided to break up again for the 15th time but he agreed to watch the apartment and her dog, Beau, while she was in Vegas before moving out. *It's fine, I'm fine. On to bigger and better things.* She was in denial and her heart was destroyed. Her world began and ended with that man and his boys. She would've continued that viciously toxic and deliciously-satisfying-in-bed relationship the rest of her life. She wanted Tanner every day, all day for the rest of her life. She knew they were bad together but she couldn't stop aching for him and loving him.

She pondered as to whether or not she was technically single while in Las Vegas. Tanner said he was packing while she was gone and the boys would leave the night she got back. But he also said he wanted to still see her and just not live with her. That man confused her constantly and was so inconsistent. In order to have a trusting and successful relationship, you need a healthy balance of strong, kind and consistent. Without having a partner to provide strength, kindness and consistency, you will feel the need to control in the areas they lack. Tanner's strength, especially mentally, was not there, which caused a lot of her need to control. And he sure as shit wasn't consistent, breaking up with her every two days. It's a shock she didn't get whiplash. How can you love someone but leave them every other day?

So was she single? She didn't know but she was half miserable and aching for him, and half feeling pissed and ready to be single. Antoinette's mom hated her mood swings and heartbreak that whole trip. It was supposed to be a Celine Dion fangirl trip with no drama or heartache. Just a mommy-daughter duo having the time of their lives, but Antoinette couldn't think of anything but Tanner.

Antoinette and her mother have a love-hate relationship. Her mom was the most generous, patient, selfless person ever when she wanted to be. She spoiled the shit out of Antoinette her entire life. They had lavish vacations, Antoinette was in five different dance classes each year, her mom bought her whole new wardrobes at the start of each school year and doted on her relentlessly. But it wasn't just with money. Her mom gave the best hugs, loved her so genuinely and provided all that she could for Antoinette growing up. They would have hooky days and go to the movies or shopping, just the girls. This was before attendance and truancy. But as a teenager, Antoinette did everything she could to be the absolute worst unintentionally. She was a terrible teenager. She was angry, promiscuous and a total bitch, but her mom took it all with grace.

However, once Antoinette grew up a little bit ready to embrace her badass mom, her mom then decided to become this very bitter, selfish, passive-aggressive person. Her mom may have also been battling some depression as well, but again, Antoinette didn't understand that battle and she didn't understand how her mom could change so much over such a short time.

All she kept thinking about every night was that he was probably "at a bonfire" with that girl or other girls while she was in Vegas. And being stuck with her mom all day prevented her from being able to flirt away her pain. While she couldn't flirt, she sure did dress like a slut, which her mom also hated—rightfully so. The night before seeing Celine, her mom also bought tickets to see Cher. If you haven't seen her in concert, you are missing out. Drags and trannies everywhere. The first time Antoinette had ever seen a man in fishnet tights was at a Cher concert in Detroit when she was eleven years old. It's always a wild and fun time at her concerts.

Antoinette wore a black see-through polka-dot lace shirt with just a black bra underneath for the Cher concert. Normally, she would wear a black tank top under to hide her tummy but she was in Vegas and on the verge of being single so there was no stopping her. The long-sleeved shirt and sexy as hell. Her bra was all black with lace down the sides. She curled her hair, wore a short leather skirt and did her makeup like she was ready for a music video with Snoop Dogg. She looked phenomenal, tummy and all.

Her petty ass made that picture her profile picture and did she get a reaction from Tanner? No, of course not, because they weren't even Facebook friends at that point (eye roll).

But she did send it to him via text and that was a mistake. Antoinette was trying to make him jealous and forgot the part where he hardly ever got jealous. *He was probably with some chick in our bed, not caring how hot I looked.*

Coming home from Vegas was enough to make her want to puke. She was ridden with anxiety the entire plane ride and car ride home. Was he even going to be home? Her palms were sweaty and stomach queasy. She did not want this. Not really. He was her best friend, the one she wanted to tell everything to. But he was crazy and so was she. You can't ever mix oil and water. *What can we do at this point?*

She walks up the steps with her suitcase and stands outside the door. Part of her is hoping he has cooked her dinner and poured a glass of wine like he has done so many times before. But another part of her is hoping he's ready to apologize and really change. Neither part of her is ready for them to be over. She stands behind the door for at least eight minutes before taking a deep breath and walking in. The wine is not poured and the dinner is not set. She walks in and sees bags of clothes and shoes lined up by the front door. Jesse's red toy organizer and Liam's desk and chair by the front door. Antoinette feels like she got hit in the gut.

She keeps walking past all the packed-up items and sees Tanner curled up on the couch with boys playing Minecraft.

Jesse runs up and hugs Antoinette. "I missed you!"

She obviously returns the sentiments and heads to the bathroom so she doesn't cry in front of him. Tanner sensed it and knocked on the door to come in. After he asks three times, she finally unlocks it. Antoinette is curled up in a ball on the floor crying. He hates when she cries.

———

When Antoinette first saw him, she was only sixteen working at a restaurant. He hung his pants low, wore his hat to the side, an embodiment of sexy to her sixteen-year-old self. He was bad news and she knew it. She was drawn to it. Joe, her boyfriend at the time, caught them sexting in the library at 9:00 A.M. during first period. Momma always raised her to break up with a man before you cheat but what about when you want both? Antoinette ditched Joe at prom to go to the Detroit Hoedown with him. Joe didn't stand a chance but her karma was most definitely coming.

They slept together that night. In his back seat. The second person she had slept with in her life already. Momma would be so ashamed. She told him she had never slept with a guy who wasn't her boyfriend before, hinting and hoping that he would go exclusive with her.

His response? "Well, tonight, I was your boyfriend."

————

Life without Tanner was impossible. Yes, logically she knew she was better off without him but she couldn't eat, sleep or breathe without him. Their apartment alone was enough to trap her thoughts. She had no life without Tanner and the boys. No Jesse on the weekends to cuddle and tickle. No Liam to help with homework. Was he even in school still? Were his grades falling behind? She had fallen so deeply for those boys. Blood or not, those boys were her heart.

Tanner would come over twice a week in the beginning and it would just be awkward. They both had their walls up but neither one of them could let go. They never touched each other either, which was surprising. She zoned out most of the nights when she was alone. She would binge TV, study and go to bed early. She hardly ate, which worked out well in her favor.

She felt like she had nothing to live for. She had never felt so deeply in love with a man before.

Antoinette felt like she would quite literally die from this heartbreak, as dramatic as that seems.

She was back to going out, partying half the week. This time, instead of with AJ, she went with Hope. She did this in part because Hope invited her but also in part because she wanted to hang on to Tanner's people in hopes that it would get her back into his life. She later found out that he hated every second of it of her hanging out with Hope. He felt betrayed by both and thought she was trying to "steal" Hope via manipulation when in reality she just wanted to hold on tight to the life they shared. After one of Antoinette and Hope's adventures, they headed to Granite City Brewing Company for some food. They were dressed to the nines, which matched the New Year's Eve event they had attended but not Granite City. They stuck out like sore thumbs in the brewing bar but they didn't care.

"Okay, so I have to tell you something and you can't be mad," Antoinette started up after the food had been delivered.

She had been itching all night to tell Hope about last night but was scared. Hope was a very equally aggressive and vocal person who didn't sugarcoat shit. At first, that's what turned Antoinette off around her but then she realized it was only because she was intimidated by it and needed to embrace it.

She continued, "Tanner and I slept together last night.... He came over and we were just watching TV and one thing led to another."

It had now been about five weeks since Tanner had moved out. Antoinette realized as she was telling Hope about this sexcapade, she was smiling. She had hope (pun intended) that things would work out between them, she really wanted them to.

"Honey, no...." Hope didn't have judgment in her face. She had sadness. But why?

"You don't want your two best friends back together?" Antoinette was puzzled.

"Honey, I saw Tanner on Thursday...."

Okay, that was after we slept together. Maybe he hadn't mentioned it.

"He was with his new girlfriend."

There were no words. There was nothing that came out of Antoinette's mouth. Tears became pools in her eyes. The pity in Hope's eyes was embarrassing enough. But Tanner had played her. Played her like a fiddle. *Had another girlfriend less than two months after we broke up, promised to try it out and sleep with me?* Who was this guy? This wasn't the Tanner she knew. She wanted to cuss him out for being a sleazeball but Hope wasn't supposed to have told her so she wasn't going to get her in trouble. He also brought the boys around this new girl. MY BOYS. Yes, she knew they weren't hers, not legally or biologically, but in her heart they were.

DING.

Another message from a random number.

"Did that old white guy with the Mexican-looking kids move out, mami?"

For fuck's sake.

Just respond, Antoinette. He won't stop bothering you until you do.

Chapter 15

Antoinette had obviously lied to *him.* She told him Tanner was away on a boys' trip with Liam and Jesse but would be back in a few days. *He* wanted to see her but that was a big "fuck no" for her and she told him so. With him knowing where she lived, she felt incredibly paranoid. She started sleeping with a knife under her pillow. How did he even find her?

She hadn't told Tanner about *him* being back and stalking her. Tanner knew bits and pieces of their relationship but she never told him the full story. *He was too empathetic and felt people's pain, I don't want him feeling my pain.* Oftentimes, when they were arguing and she ended up on the floor crying and shaking, he would remind her that even as angry as he was, he would never hit her. And whenever they discussed trauma, Tanner would tell her she suffered from beaten wife syndrome and she would cuss him out every time...*I am NOT a victim.*

While she wanted Tanner there for protection and support, she wasn't going to guilt him back. This new girl was a rebound and she knew it. It didn't make what he did right to her or the other woman but she pathetically knew deep in her heart that they were soulmates. However, since Hope had told her about the new girlfriend, she stopped talking to him and got herself a Tinder account. He would message her and she wouldn't respond. She was lost. She hadn't felt this broken since Sugar died. She felt like she was walking around with a missing limb. How could she be so stupid as to let a man have that much effect on her?

Antoinette was walking into her apartment complex from class and saw her door cracked open. *I know I locked it.* She pulled out the Swiss army knife with Tanner's name carved into it that she bought him and he didn't bring with him. What was she really going to do with that Swiss army knife? She didn't know how to fight, women normally backed off just with her bitchy words.

She pushes the door a little open and there are white rose petals everywhere. It's *him*. He only ever got her white roses. Tanner always got her colored bouquets. She starts to call Tanner and she feels hands cover her mouth and the Swiss army knife and phone are knocked out of her hand onto the ground.

Nice job, Antoinette. Way to be a strong, independent woman.

She is slowly escorted into the hallway, where she sees Beau cuddled up on the couch completely ignorant to the intrusion. *Great guard dog.* She tries to knee him in the gut like she
sees in the movies and it backfires because out of anger, he turns her around to face him and
punches her square in the face. She blacks out.

————

She's been living in Tennessee with her dad for a little over a month now and still talks to him consistently while talking to this redneck guy she met at her job. She wants to be full time with the redneck but like the Chingy song goes, something keeps pulling her back like an idiot.

She is brushing her teeth getting ready for work and a cramp hits her. She pauses and continues. Then another cramp and another cramp until the cramps are so bad, Antoinette is on the floor, sweating and keeled over in pain. The only person in the house is her stepmonster and she sure as shit is not asking her for any help. She waits there for a few minutes as the cramps start to dissipate while she tries to hold in pain induced vomit. She uses the ledge of the tub to help guide herself up and notices her khaki work pants are soaked in the lower area.

"Did I pee myself during the cramps?"

She takes off her pants to replace them and notices that it isn't urine but blood. She takes off her panties and notices deep and dark clotted blood.

She miscarried his baby that night. Blessing or curse?

————

After being knocked out, he must've carried her to the living room because Antoinette wakes up on the couch, dressed in some lingerie with a glass of wine on the coffee table in front of her. The rose petals are gone, the TV is on and her dog Beau is just lying next to her. *Must've been a dream, she tells herself.*

She double checks all the cabinets, closets and locks doors. No one is there. But neither is her phone. She feels exhausted and knowing that she checked everything properly, she just decides to go to bed. *Fuck the phone. This way neither Tanner nor he can contact me.* Antoinette falls asleep instantly with Beau by her side.

She wakes up to hands caressing her breasts. There's lips on her neck and a hard dick against her ass. The hands caressing her move lower to her ass and squeeze. *Tanner must've used his key for a booty call.* She never says no to him so she embraces it, pushing her ass against the hard dick.

"Yes, mi amor. Yes, I've missed you too."

For a curvy, non-athletic person, Antoinette jumped out of that bed like a damn Olympian.

"What in the actual fuck are you doing here!?"

She is frantic. She tries to show that she's not but *he* knows her. He knows she is panicking on the inside. She doesn't know where her phone is and she jumped out of bed so quickly, she didn't grab the knife. *Good one.*

"Mi amor, listen. I have gotten sober. For you. I came back to Michigan. For you."

Okay, if he is sober right now, then he is crazier than before.

He gets out of bed, he's naked. Antoinette is unsure what she ever saw in him because he is not attractive. Short, spiked-up, gelled-out hair, no facial hair (shit, no chest or leg hairs either) and pumpkin-tan color like a stereotypical Mexican. Oh, and his dick. His dick was like a micropenis and uncircumcised; she didn't know what to do with that thing the first time she felt it with all that extra skin! This was the first time she had seen him in over six years. She left him the day after his birthday while he was sleeping and never looked back. Despite his attempts the weeks following their breakup showing up at her house, she never saw his face again. Until today.

"Santiago, how can I know you're truly sorry and sober this time? We've been down this road so many times."

She loosens the tense on her shoulders, gets out of defense mode. *Okay, Antoinette. Play his game. You did this for four years, easy day.*

"Mi amor. I promise. We have been apart for six years, three weeks and four days. I can show you, my sexy cubi."

"My boyfriend will be home soon. You should go...but I can text you if you give me my phone back."

She takes a step closer to him, handing him his clothes. Faking facial expressions that say *I want you back too.*

"No. He is not coming back and you are not getting your phone! You take me for a fool! I have spent these last six years ready for you, watching you. You think I just started watching you when I started texting you? I watch you at Wayne State flirting with that one debate coach. I saw you at law school every night you walked back to the car at night. It was so hard not to stop you then. I watched you work at that restaurant. I watch you in the car with that old-ass man. I
watch you all the time, mi amor...."

He throws his clothes back on the floor and touches her face. His tiny dick is getting harder.

"I know he isn't coming back. I know he moved out. I know it's just us."

Fuck. I need a knife. I need a phone. I need to get the hell out of here.

"Okay, Santiago. I mean, baby. Baby. You're right. We broke up. He knew I wasn't over you and he couldn't take it. He left me when he saw your texts to me...."

Antoinette wants to vomit over each word. But she continues the lie to save her life.

"I never stopped loving you. I just don't want to get hurt again." *Laying it on a bit thick, chill out.*

As hard as she tries to act cool, she's shaking like a jackhammer with anxiety and fear.

He steps closer to her, his dick is now touching her pelvis area as they are almost even in height. His hands push the strap of her lingerie dress off her shoulder; it falls and one breast escapes. He smiles and kisses it while using his other hand to push off the second strap. The second breast escapes and her dress falls to the ground, leaving only panties. She just needs to get him distracted enough to get the knife under the pillow. She plays along, faking moans and loosening up. She slept with him countless times, escaping her body to make him happy. She is not willing to go that far this time.

"Mi amor. I've missed you. I've longed for your curves."

"I'm here."

Antoinette grabs his hand and laces it with her fingertips, then leads his hand to her ass to grasp it. He moans. *Did he shrink? He's your height. Was he always your height? Stop! Focus, Antoinette. Take charge, control this narrative.*

She leads him to the bed and tells him to lay down. He does willingly. Antoinette climbs on top of him and straddles him, panties still on, thank God. He tries to remove them.

"Not yet, baby. It's been so long, let's have some fun."

She starts to kiss his neck some more inches away from the knife, she goes to grab it slowly.... *Fuck. Where is it?!* She continues kissing while moving her hands all along the back of his head, secretly doubling as a way to look for that fucking knife.

"Looking for something?" he says between breaths.

But he knows. He knew what she was looking for. Antoinette goes to punch him or slap him or anything to get away and he grabs her wrists so fast, overpowering her. He throws her down on the floor and her head bangs the corner of the wall.

Throbbing in pain, Antoinette is holding the corner of her head and crying. Panicking like she did back then when he overpowered her. She didn't know what else to do. *I really should've taken those fucking self-defense classes.* He stands up off the bed, still naked, and walks toward her slowly. Antoinette starts to crawl, determined not to let this man take one more fucking minute of her life. She feels like she's in the middle of a Michael Myers *Halloween* film in slow motion.

He pulls her up by the ponytail and pulls his arm back to swing her but before he can, she bites. Hard. On his dick as it was swinging in her face. He drops her ponytail and falls to the ground, screaming.

"You fucking bitch. You will never change. You don't know how to just fucking submit like women are supposed to."

He is screaming at her on the ground between tears. Antoinette grabs a t-shirt and runs out the room. She grabs Beau and starts to walk toward the front door when she sees him running after her. He grabs her foot and she trips, falling down. Poor Beau is petrified and goes running out the front door.

Santiago pulls Antoinette by the feet toward the bedroom again; she is kicking and screaming each step of the way. She is in an apartment complex, for fuck's sake, somebody has to hear her.

"Shut the fuck up."

Whack. He slaps her. She hears ringing and he's putting something like a tie over her mouth, she thought all of Tanner's ties were gone. *Whack*, he slaps her again. He climbs on top of her and stares at her.

"We could've had it all, mi amor. We could've had a family, you could've had my babies...." *BAM*, slap again. "All you had to do was submit...." *SLAP*. "Why didn't you submit?" Antoinette is crying, her ears are ringing and her vision is blurry. She can't tell if that is blood or boogers draining from her nose.

Santiago takes his belt and binds her hands together. Then finds another two ties and binds each of her feet to the bed. *Fuck*. She is squirming and trying to punch or kick him but with each restraint, she loses more and more control. He slides off her panties.

"You are going to have my babies."

He starts to kiss her neck and press his hard dick on her inside hips.

Close your eyes. Just escape again. It's okay, you've done this plenty of times before.

Just when she feels like he is about to go inside of her, she hears a loud smack. She feels like he hit her again but doesn't feel any extra pain. Then she opens her watery eyes and sees him wide eyed, grasping his head. *SMACK* again and his naked Mexican ass is on the floor. Antoinette is so confused and then she looks toward the door and sees Tanner holding that damn *Detroit Tigers* baseball bat she gave him. Small little commemorative baseball bat, but hand carved and dense as hell.

In an instant, Tanner is untying her feet and hands. He gently removed the tie from her mouth and looked at her with such somber eyes.

"What are you doing here?" she asks between sobs. He didn't even have a key anymore.

"I came to pick up my ties ironically for...a date... and I saw Beau pacing in the hallways with your door cracked open. Grabbed my bat and saw this ugly ass on top of you.... Is this *him?*"

"Yes, but I'm fine. Let's just go."

He hands her some sweatpants and as they are walking out, they hear a groan coming from that pathetic pile of Mexican on the floor.

"Go to the car, call 9-1-1 and lock the doors. Do not open them for anyone except me."

"Um, what are you going to do? Just come with me. He isn't worth it."

Tanner gave her that former Navy look telling her she didn't get a say in this decision and to leave before it made her an accessory to whatever he was about to do. She listened, swiped up Beau and headed to the car.

After calling 9-1-1, she waited. And she waited. While she trusted Tanner to do some torture shit, she also knew Santiago. She knew he was clever and smart. She left Beau in the car and slowly walked up to her door. Thankfully it was still open so she slid into the kitchen and grabbed the largest kitchen knife she could find. She heard nothing but some moans and couldn't tell if they were coming from Tanner or Santiago.

She slowly tiptoed her way to the bedroom and of fucking course, Santiago had gotten the hold on Tanner and was tying him up in the corner. *He doesn't seriously think those ties will hold Tanner, does he?* She could charge now but what if he hears her? She waits by the door, butcher knife ready. She hears the police sirens and feels a sense of relief.

"Guess it's your lucky day, old man. I'll have to kill you quickly instead of slowly like I wanted."

He pulls out the carpet knife Antoinette had under her pillow. Tanner is knocked unconscious, she is unaware how Santiago got the jump on him. *Think, think, think!*

"Santiago, don't! I will go with you. Just spare him."

She slipped the butcher knife under her tits. Yes, her breasts were large enough to hold the knife underneath. The perfect disguise. The Mexican is thinking and pondering his options, holding the knife up to Tanner's neck while looking at Antoinette.

"Think about it. Deportation and prison, or we can run away together. Leave him, let's go."

After seeing that her hands are empty and Tanner is tied up, he drops the carpet knife and walks toward her. He is smiling. *He is fucking delusional. Where are the cops?* He grabs her hand and leads her to the back doors. The sirens are getting louder. They have to be parked outside by now. He stops dead in his tracks.

"Nope. I can't do it, mi amor. I have to kill him."

Santiago turns around and heads toward Tanner thinking that Antoinette is defenseless, obviously not thinking she is hiding a weapon in her braless boobs. Just as his back is fully facing her, she grabs the knife and stabs him in the right shoulder blade. She probably should've gone for his head but she has never stabbed anyone! He stops and falls, turns over and looks at her, pissed. He pulls the knife out and goes to stand up. Antoinette jumps over him, runs to the kitchen and throws the next largest one at him. It stabs him in the leg, she is no Charlie's Angel. She goes to grab another knife and the cops bust open the front door, screaming with their guns in position. She drops the knife and instantly feels relief.

Two cops handcuffed Santiago while calling for paramedics for both Tanner and Santiago. The third cop untied and woke Tanner up slowly to make sure he was okay. Once she was given the go-ahead to see Tanner, she stopped mid-statement with the other police officer and ran her little legs to him.

He was beaten badly but overall okay. She had no words to say to him. They just sat there, both bloody and bruised, hugging one another.

———

Antoinette couldn't wait to get out of that apartment after everything went down. She was staying back with her parents while working with a realtor to buy a house. She filed an official restraining order from *him* but thanks to her part-time law school education she also made sure that *he* would be going away for quite a while. Oh, and the best part? After he served his not-long-enough sentence, they were deporting his Mexican ass back to Pumpkin Land. She would rather him rot in jail than in Mexico. The only way she'd ever truly feel safe is if he was dead.

Tanner was over every night since then, worried as all hell. She knew eventually the worry and adrenaline rush would wear off and they would have to face reality. He had moved out. He had a girlfriend (or did before the Mexican attack). What did all of this mean for them? Antoinette was too exhausted to care. She was her own superhero that night and praised herself every night after that.